Fuck the Fairytale

Find Your Own Magic

By

Mandy Merrifield

Mandy Merrifield

Copyright © 2025 Mandy Merrifield

All rights reserved.

No part of this publication may be reproduced, stored in a retrieval system, or transmitted in any form or by any means, electronic, mechanical, photocopying, recording, or otherwise, without the prior written permission of the copyright owner, except for brief quotations used in reviews or scholarly work.

For my girls.

Table of Contents

Once upon a time...

Gratitude

To everyone who contributed to this book, thank you.

You shared your real stories, not the polished ones we were taught to present to the world. You showed me strength in honesty, and you helped this book become something that cuts through the quiet yet insistent noise of expectation and speaks to real life.

I did not expect this book to teach me lessons along the way; I mistakenly thought I had most things figured out.

I was wrong.

Writing this book repeatedly slapped me in the face with lessons about the fairytales I was still chasing without realising it, forcing me to own where I'd been stuck, and pushing me to choose to write a better script for myself.

To the brilliant women in my community: thank you for having my back, for calling me forward, for saying, "Of course you can do this," when I started to believe the old stories that said I couldn't, when I began to doubt myself, and when it all just felt too big. You are proof that women rewriting their lives do not do it alone.

And to my Aunty Sue, thank you for always seeing me. You have always backed my intelligence, my dreams, and what I was capable of. My tenth birthday arrived with a book from you: *Playing Beatie Bow* by Ruth Park, and I fell in love with stories. As my editor, you critiqued with the professionalism I needed, not the 'familial loving' version, and you have made this book better.

There are other strong women in my life as well, my mum, my Aunty Sandy, and my Nan (who I miss more than anything). I come from a long line of strong women, and I know that my daughters are the next chapter in these generations of strength.

To my girls, I hope you never feel the need to shrink or soften who you are to make others comfortable. I hope you back yourselves fully, trust your instincts, and never wait to be chosen when you can choose yourselves. Chase what lights you up; you may fall, but you will rise, and you will define what happiness looks like on your own terms. May you always remember that you come from generations of powerful women, and now, you get to decide what that power looks like for you.

This book is my heart on my sleeve for you both. You are my world.

I hope this book does what so many women deserve: to take up space in your life exactly how you want, and to be more in control of your own damn story. I hope it nudges you to question the rules, push back on the expectations, and choose yourself, without waiting for permission.

Thank you, all of you, for helping me flip the script, question the rules, and write a story that doesn't wait for a happily ever after; it builds one.

Thank you for being part of a story that is not about finding magic, it is about owning it.

Mandy Merrifield

You know what?

I don't know whether I ever actually wanted the fairytale. Not really. Not in the rational, logical, conscious way we tell ourselves we make decisions.

When I was a teenager, about fifteen, maybe sixteen, I was convinced I was independent. Worldly, even. I thought I was so damn mature. I had opinions about everything. I wore my self-assurance like armour. And for what reason? I have no idea. I had never even left the east coast of Australia. My greatest rebellion was probably wearing school shorts instead of a dress and thinking I was popular because I was one of the first in my school year to have a car.

It was a Datsun 200B.

Get real, Mandy.

I was so sure I was nothing like my parents; that I was destined for something more glamorous, more exciting, more… big.

The ordinary suburban life I saw around me, weekly grocery shopping, bills, the same dinner menu on repeat, chores and washing up, routines and sameness, felt suffocating, dull, monotonous.

I couldn't possibly want that, could I?

But here's the thing.

That glittering imaginary picture, that promise of what the future will look like: the diamond ring offered by your Prince Charming while he kneels before you; the highly paid job where you're looked up to and admired, walking in heels that click confidently down a polished hallway; the perfect, romantic relationship that whispers of 'happily ever after'; the tidy home that smells like candles and looks like a spread from *Home Beautiful*, somehow, somewhere, that narrative gets under your skin. It creeps into your psyche before you even know it's there. You don't remember inviting it in, yet it still finds a way to take up residence.

A modern-day fairytale, if you will.

Fuck the Fairytale: Find Your Own Magic

But where does it come from, that quiet conditioning that tells us this, and only this, is what success, love, and happiness look like?

It is so easy to point the finger at social media these days, the endless scroll of highlight reels, the perfectly curated feeds, the filters, the lighting, the matching sets of linen sheets, the unblemished selfies captioned with faux humility.

In today's world, we are fed stories of perfection in tiny square boxes, lives edited for aesthetic appeal. It is so tempting to think social media is where it comes from, this longing for a fairytale life.

But truth be told, I grew up in the 1980s and 1990s. Social media wasn't a thing then. Our idols weren't influencers; they were characters in movies and on glossy magazine covers, the women we saw portrayed in the media who seemed to have it all together.

So, if it's not Instagram or TikTok, where does my fairytale come from?

Dare I say it… the patriarchy?

And if I do say this, are you immediately rolling your eyes, assuming this is about to turn into some fiery feminist monologue? Are you bracing yourself for the part where I rant about gender inequality and tear down the institution of marriage with unrelenting fury?

My darling reader, please don't. That is not the plan.

This book isn't a manifesto or a diatribe, it is an invitation.

A conversation.

A reflection on what happens when we start to realise that maybe, just maybe, the story we've been sold doesn't actually belong to us.

The intention of the pages ahead is simple: design a life that feels good to you.

That's it.

Simple.

No rules.

No shoulds.

No good-girl checklists.

Just you, writing your own story.

Because truly.

Fuck the Fairytale.

Throw it out the window. Burn it if you must. The original fairytale script was never written with you in mind anyway. It was written to keep you small, palatable, and predictable. It was written to make you think you needed rescuing, instead of realising you already held the pen.

So, what happens if instead, you write your own damn story?

What if you pick the parts that feel good, the parts of the romance, the dreams, the magic, and then discard everything else that doesn't serve you?

What is this 'everything else' I'm referring to?

You know the answer to that, darling girl.

It is the expectations. The pressures. The judgements that are thrown at women from every direction. The silent scorecards that keep us striving and comparing.

Because here's the truth: the fairytale was never the problem. The problem was believing it had to look a particular way,

That there was one script, one timeline, and one happy ending.

But what if your story looks nothing like that happy ending, and it's still enough? Or even, what if it is more than you had ever hoped for?

Throughout this book, you are going to meet incredible women. Women who have lived, loved, lost, and rebuilt. Women who have chased the fairytale until it broke them, and women who have run from it like their lives depended on it. You'll meet the ones who fought to defend it, even when it didn't fit anymore, and the ones who burned it to the ground and started again from the ashes.

Fuck the Fairytale: Find Your Own Magic

Each of them will tell you something different. Each of them will hold a mirror to a different version of yourself.

Some of their stories will make you laugh. Some might make you cry. But all of them, I hope, will make you pause, just long enough to ask: what would my story look like if I wrote it for myself?

Because, my love, that is what is at the heart of it.

You get to choose.

You get to decide what success looks like.

You get to define 'happily ever after.'

You get to say 'this is enough,' even if the world tells you otherwise.

And maybe that is what growing up really is, not rebellion for the sake of being different, not chasing independence to prove we can, but learning that freedom is quieter.

Growing up is choosing your own life, on your own terms, without apology.

It is sitting in the messiness, the magic, the contradiction of it all, and saying: "This, this is mine, and these are my choices."

Maybe, just maybe, the fairytale isn't something to reject outright.

Maybe it's something to rewrite.

To evolve.

To soften around the edges until it feels like home again.

But please, my darling, let it be *your* version of home, not anyone else's.

So, as you turn these pages, keep an open mind and an open heart. Let the stories meet you where you are. Take what resonates, and leave what does not.

Use these stories as threads to weave your own tapestry, a life that feels like *you.*

Not your mother's version. Not your friend's version. Not society's version.

Yours.

Because you're allowed to build a life that feels beautiful from the inside out, not just one that photographs well.

You're allowed to be messy, powerful, tender, ambitious, and uncertain, and to do all of these things at once.

You're allowed to want love *and* independence, comfort *and* adventure, softness *and* strength.

You're allowed to have it all, but just make sure, darling girl, that your version of *all* is defined by you.

So, take a deep breath.

Let go of the script.

And let's begin.

Chapter 1:
The Fairytale Unwrapped

Unknowingly, and certainly unconsciously, I spent years chasing the fairytale.

The version of life that looked good on paper. The one that made people nod approvingly and say, "She's doing it right."

I had the things that were supposed to matter, the markers of a life well lived, or at least, a life that photographed well. A beautiful, almost matching pair of flaxen-haired daughters. A good-looking, reliable husband, a provider type, with a square jaw and an enviable head of hair. You know the kind: tall, dark, and handsome. The kind that looks like he stepped straight out of a casting call for the ideal man.

We had the beige house in the suburbs (technically off-white, but close enough), the right postcode, the respectable cars, the decent income, the holiday place down the coast. All the milestones that were meant to add up to happiness.

But underneath, something just wasn't right.

And that's the thing about fairytales: they can look perfect from the outside. They can tick all the boxes, line up neatly in a row, and still, somehow, one plus one refuses to add up to two.

The idea of a life that ticks all of the boxes is comforting. It is predictable. It gives us a sense of safety, almost as if by following the map, we'll never get lost. But here's the truth that most of us figure out too late: the map was never drawn for us. It was drawn for the world's convenience.

Fairytales are not real.

They are stories written to keep us entertained, hopeful, and compliant.

And the authors? Mostly men: Hans Christian Andersen, the Brothers Grimm, Charles Perrault, Aesop. Men wove morality lessons into myth and sold them as truth.

So, let's start with one of the most iconic: *Sleeping Beauty.*

We were told she was the lucky one, beautiful, adored, chosen, protected.

Everything a good girl should aspire to be.

But then she made a mistake.

And what happens when a woman makes a mistake? She is punished.

Sleeping Beauty's crime was curiosity. She touched the wrong thing, the spindle, and for that, she was condemned to silence.

One touch, and she fell. Not dead. Just asleep. Frozen in time. Suspended between what was and what could have been.

She didn't scream. She didn't fight. She just… stopped.

And that is the part of the fairytale we were told was romantic. The stillness. The waiting. The idea that a woman's most desirable state is passive, silent, and waiting to be saved.

How many of you know that place? That quiet, heavy, waiting place.

Maybe you've been there.

Maybe you're there now.

Maybe you've been in a relationship that looks perfect on the outside but feels hollow when the lights go off.

Maybe you've been in a job that pays well but drains the colour from your days.

Maybe you've been the dependable one, the peacemaker, the one who never rocks the boat.

And somewhere deep down, you know something is missing, but it's too hard to fight, too hard to leave, too hard to change.

So instead, you stay.

You settle.

You tell yourself it's fine. It's not that bad. It's probably just a phase.

Fuck the Fairytale: Find Your Own Magic

You tell yourself that maybe it's better, safer, certainly easier, to just put up with it.

Because somewhere along the line, we were taught that being quiet was virtuous. That patience was power. That if we were kind enough, grateful enough, good enough, then something, or someone, would eventually come along to make it all worthwhile.

We were taught that our reward for endurance would be love.

That our waiting would be worth it.

That we would be rescued.

Phew.

What a relief, right?

Except… what happens when the rescue never comes?

What happens when you realise no one is coming? That the silence you've been living in isn't peace, it's paralysis.

That's the part of the story no one talks about. The part that never made it into the bedtime version.

What isn't written on the page is the weight of it, the heaviness that settles over you when you've silenced yourself for too long.

That romanticised sleep is, in reality, suffocation.

Sometimes that heaviness drops suddenly, a heartbreak, a betrayal, a realisation that cracks your world open. Other times, it builds quietly over years, almost imperceptibly. One compromise at a time. One unspoken truth. One too many swallowed 'no'.

Until one day, you wake up, and you don't recognise yourself anymore.

You're not unhappy, exactly. But you're not alive either.

You're… fine.

And *fine* is the most dangerous place of all.

Because *fine* is the place where dreams go to die slowly, the place between asleep and awake, where you convince yourself that this is enough because it is easier than wanting more.

You stop asking questions. You stop making noise. You stop wanting.

And the world applauds you for it.

'You're so grounded.'

'You're so lucky.'

'You've got everything anyone could want.'

But do you? Do you really?

Or are you, in fact, hemmed in? An invisible ring fence, if you will. Not visible to the outside world, not something made of bricks and mortar, but something just as real.

What is your fence made of? We all have one. That imperceptible barrier that keeps us from pushing too far, asking for too much, being *too* anything.

Maybe yours is made of words you've heard all your life.

'Be grateful.'

'Don't rock the boat.'

'You should be happy.'

'You're too much.'

'You've got what everyone wants.'

'What more do you need?'

Maybe your fence is built from expectations, fear, or exhaustion.

Maybe it's built on the quiet belief that you're not allowed to want more, not when you already have so much.

And maybe you've started to push, ever so slightly, against it.

Maybe, as you read this, you can feel a faint vibration in your chest, the tiniest spark of rebellion whispering, "What if there's more?"

Fuck the Fairytale: Find Your Own Magic

Or maybe you're still asleep.

Maybe your eyes are fluttering, but you're not quite ready to wake up yet.

And that's okay.

Awakening is not an event; it's a process. It's uncomfortable and inconvenient. It often comes at the worst possible time.

But it is also beautiful.

Because the moment you start to question the story, *your* story, you begin to reclaim it.

You remember that your voice matters.

That your desires, wants, and needs are not dangerous.

That your mistakes do not make you unworthy.

Sleeping Beauty didn't need a prince to wake her. She needed her own permission to open her eyes.

And maybe that's what we're all doing, in our own way.

Waking up.

Slowly, clumsily, sometimes painfully.

Learning that the fairytale isn't about rescue at all, it's about resurrection.

It's about the parts of ourselves that we put to sleep long ago, finally stirring, stretching, and asking to be seen again.

Do you remember Sleeping Beauty's mistake? Of course you do, she touched the spindle, pricked her finger, and then fell into a deep sleep.

Tell me: what was your spindle?

What was the thing that pricked you just enough to make you stop?

Was it the heartbreak that cracked open your illusions?

The career that left you empty?

The motherhood that swallowed your identity whole?

The slow erosion of yourself in service to everyone else's comfort?

Whatever it was, I want you to know this: you can wake up.

You don't need permission.

You don't need a prince.

You just need to decide that your story isn't over yet.

Because maybe, just maybe, the fairytale was never meant to end at 'happily ever after.'

Maybe the real story begins in the moment you choose to open your eyes and quietly say: *no more.*

No more silence.

No more pretending.

No more waiting for someone else to change your life.

Because this time, the kiss that wakes you will come from within.

From your courage.

From your clarity.

From the knowing that you deserve a life that feels like yours, not one that merely looks perfect on paper.

So, if you are reading this and your heart is thudding just a little faster, that thud is your soul stirring, my darling girl. That heartbeat you can feel, stronger and more insistent in your chest, is the beginning of your awakening.

And when you're ready, truly ready, you'll lower the drawbridge, step out of the castle, and write your next chapter.

Not the one the world expects.

The one that finally feels true.

Guin: Reclaiming Me

The Life I Was Told to Want

I grew up in Canberra, the land of cul-de-sacs, home ownership, and public servants.

The streets all looked the same: modest brick homes, well-kept lawns, sensible cars, and the constant hum of people working government jobs they didn't hate enough to quit.

It wasn't glamorous, but it was stable.

Predictable.

And that was the dream.

My parents were part of that crowd, suburban, steady, dependable public servants; most of my friends' parents were the same.

The thought that life could be lived another way never entered my imagination; no one stated there were other paths; the script never hinted at an alternative.

You went to school, got a government job, bought a house, married someone decent, had kids, took them to swimming lessons and sports, and kept the machine running.

That was it.

That was the story I was told, not through words, but through monotonous routine and example.

Through every before and after school care drop-off.

Through every 'you'll be right' when I complained.

Through every adult conversation that ended with mortgage rates and who got promoted.

And I believed it.

I thought that was what life was supposed to be: suburbia, routine, financial stability.

And a socially suitable level of exhaustion.

I never asked myself if it was what I actually wanted.

Wanting wasn't part of the equation.

The goal wasn't joy; it was making it work.

So I did what was expected. I went into the public service, and I even got excited about it. At nineteen, I landed a job in a call centre and felt like I'd made it.

A real job in the Australian Public Service! Woohoo!

Except… when I told people, they said, "Oh, well, it's not really a public service job if it's in a call centre."

That stung.

It was my first taste of the quiet hierarchy built into the dream; you could tick all the right boxes and still not be enough.

But I didn't question the system. I just kept going.

I bought the nice suburban house.

I married the man.

I went to work and put my daughter in care because that's what everyone else did.

I felt the push from bosses, friends, and family, all telling me to work more, earn more, achieve more.

Be more.

And all the while, the mums around me were doing everything on their own.

Driving from swimming lessons to sports to school functions, managing to hold it all together, which often included a paid job that had to straddle the myriad of responsibilities of the everyday.

All the while, their husbands worked more and continued to disappear into a land built singularly on career, promotions, and status.

No one asked if we were happy.

The assumption was that if you had the house, the job, the kid, and the chaos, you had won.

When the Fairytale Started to Crack

The funny thing about the right life is that it starts to itch before it collapses.

For me, the cracks started quietly, on those long family drives where I'd scroll real estate listings for old churches, tiny cottages, and small blocks out of town.

I would drag my husband along to look at them on weekends, imagining a slower life, a bigger garden, air that didn't smell like bureaucracy.

He didn't want it. That was not part of his picture.

He wanted the dream: new cars, big mortgage, kids in before and after school care, everything shiny, within a 15-minute radius of the polished, expected, and predictable bureaucracy.

I tried to convince myself I wanted it too. But every time I came home to our suburban house with its chickens and veggie patch, those vegies and chooks being the only things that felt like me, I would still feel a tug of resistance, a tug of unhappiness.

And then we moved.

Out of the suburbs, and closer to the bureaucracy.

Out of the house and into an apartment.

No yard, no chickens, no space.

Just city noise and walls that closed around me.

And that is when it hit me.

Hard.

This wasn't my life.

It was a life built on other people's expectations.

A hand-me-down dream.

And it didn't fucking fit.

I remember the sadness of small moments.

Taking my daughter to swimming lessons every week without her dad. Driving home past all the families who looked happy, and wondering why I couldn't make normal work for me.

The realisation came gradually, but it built into a solid, tangible reality: everyone else's version of happiness was killing me.

Everything I'd been told to want, the job title, the mortgage, the family setup, the image, none of it made me happy.

I was ticking boxes on someone else's checklist.

And I was exhausted.

There's a thing that happens when you start unravelling the fairytale.

You lose your place in the story.

You start seeing the cracks in your own reflection, and that's terrifying, because you see how much of your identity was built around being the good one. The responsible one. The one who did things properly.

Waking up cost me a lot.

Emotionally, socially, personally.

It meant letting go of the marriage that looked right on paper.

It meant facing the version of myself that was complicit in my own unhappiness.

And it meant hearing the quiet judgments, the whispered "what happened?", the "she just threw it all away."

But I didn't throw anything away.

I walked away.

There is a difference.

Leaving the Fairytale Behind

I left my husband.

There are big reasons, the kind that don't need to be aired for public consumption. But when I left, I knew I was done living for appearances.

I packed up my life, my kid, and my sanity, and moved over three hours away from my Canberra life.

I bought a house with a mortgage that didn't make my chest tighten every time I saw the bank statement. Two acres of actual space. More chickens than anyone could need. A garden that grew food instead of just sucking up water.

Now, today, instead of pretending, I am living.

I have a husband who actually likes being with me.

A husband who puts family first.

Our kids don't go to before or after school care. We take turns to be there for breakfast, and we hang out in the afternoon.

We don't have fancy cars, a massive house, or proximity to a Westfield shopping mall.

What we have is peace.

It takes thirty minutes to get to the nearest big grocery store.

I love that.

It means we're far enough away from the noise. Far enough away that when I walk outside, I can breathe.

I work on a contract-to-contract basis, covering maternity leave, short-term roles, local councils, schools, and even mining companies. And I love it. Every job teaches me something new, and I leave it better than I found it. I no longer need a career ladder. I don't need to chase promotions or permanent roles or a gold service pin for surviving another decade of bureaucracy.

Instead, I negotiate my life around what matters: time with my family.

I can be there before and after school.

I can say no to nonsense.

And the freedom that comes with that? It is addictive.

I've returned to university, completed a postgraduate certificate, and am now working towards a Master's degree.

Not because I have to, but because I want to.

Because I can.

And because it is mine.

The fairytale told me happiness was about climbing the ladders of job grades, pay scales, and property.

The truth is, I found my happiness by stepping off that ladder.

What Freedom Actually Feels Like

Freedom isn't always pretty.

It isn't the postcard version: wine glass in hand, sunset on the verandah, breeze on your face, golden light spilling over everything. Sometimes it looks like that, sure. Mostly, it just feels like breathing again.

Freedom is simple.

It is slow mornings with a coffee in the backyard, the kids barefoot and chasing the chickens.

It is sitting in silence after the kids have gone to bed, not because you're drained, but because you are content.

Freedom is working hard, not for validation, but to build something that feels right: to provide, to grow, and to live on your own terms.

It is knowing that if a workplace doesn't align with my values, I can walk away. That if something feels wrong, I can change it.

Freedom isn't about escaping responsibility; it is about choosing which responsibilities actually deserve you.

But the fairytale does not die quietly, even after you have consciously and very deliberately walked away from it.

Sometimes, I still feel the anxiety creep in.

The fear that I'm not doing it right.

The fear that I don't have enough job security.

The fear that I have veered too far left of centre, too far from what is normal.

That voice, the one that says, "You should have stayed, you should have done it properly," still shows up now and then.

I have learned to talk back.

I talk to my husband, to my friends, to the people who actually see me. They remind me of what I have done and what I have achieved. They roll their eyes at my doubts and say with so much love in their hearts, "Guin, you're amazing. You've built a life from the ground up."

They are right.

I forget that sometimes.

I forget how many times I've hit the end of a contract only to have multiple job offers waiting for me.

I forget how good I am at what I do.

I forget how many versions of myself I have outgrown.

The lesson isn't about never doubting; it is about not letting the doubt take the wheel.

The Realisation That Changed Everything

When I left that old life, I didn't just leave a marriage or a house.

I left a system that said women should do it all and still be grateful.

I left a story that told me my worth was measured by how well I could keep spinning plates while maintaining a smile on my face.

Now, I live slowly.

I know my neighbours.

I know which chooks lay which eggs.

My daughter walks down to the creek, and I don't panic.

There is a peace in that, in knowing that the life I live isn't glossy or perfect, but it is mine.

And that is what the fairytale got wrong all along.

It wasn't supposed to be about fitting in.

It is supposed to be about feeling free.

Being Brave

Growing up, love wasn't something I saw done well.

My parents slept in separate rooms. My in-laws did too.

They would go on holidays without each other, come back, and pretend that everything was fine, normal even.

So I thought that was just what relationships looked like: polite distance with a side of resentment.

You didn't talk about what you wanted; you just accepted that this was as good as it was going to get.

You went through the motions: kids, a house, a shared bank account, and called it a partnership.

No one ever said you were meant to like your partner. You just had to tolerate them.

Fuck the Fairytale: Find Your Own Magic

It took me years to understand *that* wasn't love. It took years to understand that I was allowed to look at what my parents had and bravely say, "I don't want that."

Real love, I have learned, is friendship first.

Sometimes you're the best of friends, sometimes you're not, but you still choose each other every day.

Real love is not about settling; it is about showing up.

Real love, for yourself and of yourself, is being brave enough to say, "this isn't working," and also being brave enough to stay when it is.

My first marriage looked right from the outside.

The wedding, the house, the kid, the full-time jobs; the whole good life brochure.

But behind the photos, it was dreadful.

He would say horrible things about me, about my body, in front of other people. And they would laugh. Like it was normal, as if humiliation was simply a regular part of being married.

Once, a woman actually called him out. She told him to stop. He didn't like that.

He cut her and her husband out of our lives completely.

That was how my first husband handled being challenged: erase anyone who noticed the cracks.

Back then, I didn't see it for what it was. I was so busy trying to keep the image together that I ignored the rot underneath.

Eventually, I could no longer pretend.

The story I had built around us collapsed. And when it did, I saw the truth: I had been treated so poorly, for so long, that I could not even remember what respect felt like.

When I finally left, he messaged me and said something along the lines of, "I hope your new boyfriend gives you everything you need, like *this* and *that* and the *other*…"

And it broke me.

Because I then saw that for the *entirety* of our marriage, I had been telling him what I needed, what I wanted, what would make me joyful, and what respect and love looked like to me.

I had told him openly, over and over, again and again.

He had taken no notice, or perhaps he just hadn't cared.

I had tried to meet his every need and bend myself to fit his comfort.

But he had never done the same.

Not once.

That was the moment I promised myself I would never beg for love again.

Redefining the Fairytale

Love

Now? Love is easy in the ways that matter and challenging in the ways that count.

My husband now, my forever husband, is the kind of person I never knew existed.

He's not perfect, but he is kind.

He is steady.

He shows up.

We have built our life together like teammates, not adversaries.

Do we still bicker? Sometimes.

But there's no cruelty, no scorekeeping, no pretending.

And we talk it out.

And because I finally believe I'm worth more, I treat myself in a way that shows I know I am worth every goddamn morsel of love, respect, kindness, fun, dignity, and silliness available to me, and then everything else in between as well.

That is what changes everything. When you realise your worth is no longer negotiable.

Career

I grew up thinking success was simple maths: a public service job *plus* a mortgage *plus* a new car *plus* an overseas holiday *equals* success.

That was the formula everyone followed.

You worked hard, saved, bought a home, went to Bali every couple of years, and you told yourself you were comfortable.

Comfort, I have learned, is nothing more than a trap; when all it is built on are footings made of stress, pressure, and expectation.

Success looks different to me today.

Comfort is time in my garden.

It is being there and present for my kids.

Ease is not waking up with a knot in my chest because a mortgage payment is due.

I still work, and I work hard. But it's on my terms, mostly contract roles. And when the contract is done, when the project is delivered, I walk away without apology.

When I left the city and my respectable life, I defied every expectation people had for me, and every fear I had for myself.

Leaving my husband.

Riding a motorbike.

Having a baby outside of marriage.

Marrying again.

Taking contract jobs instead of stable ones.

Moving too far away from the centre of bureaucracy, the expected setting that my life had been built on.

I did all of these things.

Everyone had a belief.

I got told, over and over, that I was making mistakes. But every so-called mistake made me freer. Every time I walked away from something that didn't fit, I got closer to myself.

And I came to understand something powerful: I don't want the gold watch, or the Sunday afternoon barbecue brag about who earns more, or the inevitable job level comparisons and passive-aggressive competition.

I want flexibility.

I want family.

I want a life that breathes.

That is what success looks like now.

Body

In the 80s and 90s, every woman I knew was on a diet. Mums, teachers, even the uber-cool media personalities.

My mum did the diets, and my dad ran commentary on her body and her eating habits.

Kate Moss told the world, "Nothing tastes as good as skinny feels."

So, of course, that got under my skin.

I learned early that a woman's body was something to be managed, criticised, and joked about.

My ex-husband sure didn't help.

He would make comments about my body in public, at friends' barbecues, and in front of people.

The kind of comments that make you shrink into yourself.

Fuck the Fairytale: Find Your Own Magic

But here's the thing: people see more than you think.

Once, a friend of mine, who is a bra fitter, laughed at him when he made some shitty remark about my boobs. She looked him dead in the eye and said something that shut him right up. And you know what? She's seen way more tits than he ever has.

That moment stuck with me.

Because for the first time, someone didn't let him define me.

Now, I see my body differently.

My body is not a project. It's not a punchline. It's mine.

It's grown and fed beautiful kids. It runs, it moves, it works hard.

My forever husband loves it, which is a nice change.

More importantly, I love it.

My friends aren't body-obsessed or competitive. We don't sit around comparing or tearing each other down. We build each other up.

Running has helped me reclaim my body, to focus on what it can do, not how it looks.

And so did something else I never thought I'd do: I did a boudoir photo shoot.

Standing there in front of the camera and seeing the photos afterwards, it was both confronting and emotional.

I cried.

Because for the first time, I saw myself as I really am.

Not the distorted version I'd carried in my head.

In my opinion, any woman who has ever hated her body should do one.

It is expensive, but it is worth every damn cent.

Mandy Merrifield

Family

Being a good woman was never meant to be about being obedient. But that is certainly how it was framed: be polite, be kind, be selfless. Be what others need you to be.

Fuck that.

Being good isn't about fitting into other people's expectations.

It is about being true.

Being kind, but not at your own expense.

It is about treating people well because it is who you are, not because you want approval or to be performative.

When I left my ex-husband, he did something that still stings me to this day.

He started spending time with my parents, having lunch with my dad, and building relationships that made it harder for me to feel like I could go home.

One day, I called my dad and asked if he wanted to catch up.

He said no, he already had lunch plans with a friend.

The friend was my ex-husband.

Something broke in me that day, in that instant, in that 'no' from my dad.

I realised that I'd been pushed out of my own family circle, not because they didn't love me, but because they didn't understand what was really happening.

So I distanced myself.

I had to.

And once I did, my ex-husband lost interest in his little game; he had achieved what he set out to do. But for me, the damage was done. The intangible, invisible distance was there within my family, and even now, it still hurts.

Fuck the Fairytale: Find Your Own Magic

Occasionally, my mum still suggests I move back, back to the suburbs. I love her, but I have learned to stand firm.

I no longer negotiate when it comes to my happiness.

Nor do I negotiate the shape and company of my immediate family.

After having my first daughter, I swore I would never do it again. I would never have any more children, and I meant it.

I even started donating my eggs to help others have children.

People tried to talk me out of donating eggs; they said it wasn't right and that I would regret it.

And I would look them straight in the eye and say, "My body, my choice."

That usually shut them up. Or made them furious, which I think was even better.

I loved babies; what I didn't love was the version of motherhood I had experienced.

Then I met my forever husband.

And suddenly, I realised that it wasn't that I didn't want more kids.

It was so obvious; the thing that had been quietly weighing on me, shaping my decisions: I didn't want more kids with the wrong person, and that was the thought that had been running my show.

Now, we've got our kids together, and our family doesn't talk about halves or steps. We don't split love like it's a math problem.

Everyone is family, full stop.

Our town is tiny, less than five hundred people, and it is home.

People here don't gossip for sport. They care, they check in, but they give space.

They are 'Team Guin'; they love me, call me out when I'm being dramatic, and they even tell me when my pants are unflattering, camel toe and all.

That is real love.

When I left my ex-husband, I was embarrassed. I didn't tell people right away. But when I finally opened up about my experience in that marriage, I started to appreciate how many of my friends had been living in the same quiet misery. We had all been hiding, ashamed, and thinking we were the only ones.

Now, those same women are my family. The women who would show up at midnight if I needed them.

My daughter once walked to school from her dad's house and felt scared on the way. She ducked into a coffee shop, and within seconds, five women I know stepped in to take care of her. They got her to school safely, then called me to let me know what had happened.

That is the kind of community I have made around me. A place where my kids are safe because they're known, and because the women around us are strong and kind and look out for each other.

That is the fairytale I never got told about, the one that most of us didn't know existed, and it is the one I have fought for and built for myself.

The Magic of a Life You Choose

I don't really subscribe to religion, but I do believe in something bigger.

In kindness.

In connection.

In the quiet magic of a good cup of coffee and a day that feels full.

I've walked away from a lot: stable jobs, a respectable life, and all of the people in that world who didn't get it.

But I've walked towards something truer.

For me, freedom looks like this:

If a workplace doesn't feel safe, I can quit that day without panicking.

If a boss crosses a line, I call it out.

If something doesn't align with my values, I don't swallow it.

That is power. Not control, but choice.

What makes me happy now?

Slow weekends. Bushwalks. Coffee with my husband. Watching our kids grow up wild and kind.

I am happy knowing that I have built a life that doesn't require me to pretend.

We will travel again one day.

I'll study some more.

But for now, this quiet, grounded, messy, joyful life; this is it.

This is what the fairytale should have been all along.

Not about looking perfect.

About feeling free.

Mandy Merrifield

A love letter to my younger self

Girl, slow down.

Follow your heart, and by that I mean, not the clichés, but your own dreams.

Don't fall in love fast.

Protect your heart, and know that friends are worth more than lovers.

Have fun, but think about where you want to be in life, not where someone else wants you to be.

You are the only one who knows what you want, so do your best to make sure you are making decisions that won't fuck it up for you in the future.

But if you do, forgiveness will be there.

Anytime you are feeling down, know that I love you, that you love yourself, and on the darkest days, I promise there is sunshine ahead.

Focus on the silver linings.

Love you,

Guinny

Chapter 2:
Whose Story Am I Living?

For me, like most women, the fairytale trap started early.

Barbie with her Dreamhouse. Disney princesses with their wide-eyed innocence and flowing gowns. Picture books where the story always ends with the girl being chosen, claimed, or rescued. The reward for her patience, her kindness, her beauty, or even her sacrifice was always the same: a man, a castle, a crown, a happily-ever-after.

Did you eat it up as much as I did?

I bet you did.

We didn't stand a chance, did we? From the moment we could hold a hairbrush and call it a microphone, we were serenading a version of life that promised adoration and security in exchange for compliance and grace.

Barbie didn't pay the mortgage or clean the Dreamhouse.

Ariel gave up her voice for love.

Cinderella was rewarded for her quiet servitude, not her courage.

Snow White was asleep when she got her big break.

And somewhere, deep in our subconscious, the message stuck: if you're good, patient, pretty, and kind, life will reward you.

Here is the reality: we grew up imagining the dress, the proposal, the career that looked shiny on LinkedIn, the house with a kitchen island and bifold French doors opening onto a perfectly landscaped backyard. We didn't imagine queues, mortgage stress, toxic bosses, or the creeping, vast loneliness that comes when your real life looks nothing like the fairytale script.

The reality of my fairytale?

I wasn't happy.

And for the longest time, I couldn't even say that out loud. Because to do so would make me sound ungrateful.

Spoiled.

Difficult.

But deep down, there was a quiet ache, the kind that hums underneath the noise of everyday life. The kind that whispers, 'this can't be it.'

So, let me ask you something.

What does the fairytale mean to you?

Maybe it's the relationship. The marriage. The babies. The house in the suburbs, or perhaps the beach house, or the glittering city apartment that smells faintly of vanilla candles and ambition.

Maybe it's the big yard with a garden, or a golden retriever with a name that sounds like a wine label.

Maybe it's the career: the pencil skirt, the Manolos, the glass office, and the job title, each proving to the world that you have made it.

For most women, the fairytale is some combination of those things: Wife. Mother. Homeowner. Career woman. All perfectly coiffed, all seamlessly blended, all balanced on a knife's edge of expectation.

Smooth sailing, right?

Domestic bliss.

The highlight reel.

No hiccups. No exhaustion. No sleepless nights with screaming babies. No mention of the dysfunctional extended families or passive-aggressive in-laws. No never-ending housework.

No inner conflict between who you are and who you thought you would be.

Reality rarely, if ever, fits the picture we had in our heads.

And if someone asks? Rarely do we speak the truth.

Why?

Because silence is golden.

Because we are told, "It won't be like this forever."

Because somewhere, deep down, we still believe the reward is coming, that one day it will all click into place, and we will finally feel the contentment we were promised.

So we keep waiting. And we keep pretending. We tell ourselves it's fine. Everyone else seems fine, so we had damn well better be fine too.

That is what we see, after all, in Hollywood movies, in glossy magazines, on social media. The perfect angles. The curated smiles. The filters that soften reality until it's palatable.

But lately, something is shifting.

The tide is turning.

Women are beginning to speak. To share the unfiltered versions of their lives. To say the quiet things out loud. We are seeing posts about burnout, motherhood, loneliness, marriage fatigue, identity loss, resentment, and grief.

The raw, unglamorous truth behind the highlight reel.

But even when the truth is told, it is framed as a confession. The rhetoric goes something like this:

'I admit, I was struggling.'

'I admit, I don't have it all together.'

The subtext: we have failed.

Why does it have to be an admission?

Why does it reek of guilt?

Because the story we were told is still running in the background, humming along and telling us that we are meant to handle it all, beautifully, effortlessly, and without complaint.

We are never meant to drop the ball.

And if we do, we are told to pick it up with a smile.

Here's the thing, though: who on earth has their shit together?

No one. Not a single one of us.

Let me tell you a story.

My friend Rebecca just phoned me. I texted her at 7am this morning; it is now after 6pm. It's Saturday. She has worked all week. Two teenagers, both quiet, both glued to screens. End of the netball season. Rebecca has been looking forward to a night out with a friend, the one bright spot in a long, messy week. She planned it weeks ago, coordinating logistics with her husband so that everything would run smoothly.

But today? Nothing went to plan.

An unexpected house visitor in the morning. A sports presentation in the afternoon. Housework, bathroom cleaning, and a week's worth of washing. And a few other random curveballs thrown in, the house is undergoing renovations, just for good measure.

Then her husband announces, "I have to work today."

Cue the plot twist.

So she did it all.

Every single thing.

And it was hot, the kind of heat that melts your patience before midday.

By the time she called me, she was frazzled, running late for her evening out, determined to enjoy herself but barely holding on.

Now, you might say, "Come on. That's just normal life stuff. It all worked out. She's still going out."

Sure.

And you could also say: "It's not her husband's fault he had to work."

For sure. I hear you. This is not a dig at him. It is not that he doesn't work hard at home and at work, it is not that he hasn't put long hours into the house renovations, it is not that he is not appreciative of the way Rebecca holds everything together and provides him with a loving and stable home.

But, in Rebecca's shoes, imagine that level of juggling, day after day, year after year, with no break, no applause, no reset button.

In a more generalised sense, imagine the thousand micro-responsibilities that pile up on a woman's shoulders simply because she's better at multitasking, or she keeps everything running.

It is expected. It is the script. And it takes a toll.

Does this fairytale trap sound familiar?

The invisible framework, the forcefield, the fence that hems us in, the one made up of cultural, emotional, and psychological conditioning that teaches women to build their lives around expectations rather than desires, around approval instead of being real.

Let's play a little game of 'what if.'

What if Rebecca had said no?

No to the errands. No to last-minute changes in plans. No to carrying everyone else's load.

What would have happened?

Guilt.

Big time.

Guilt for the unwashed uniforms. Guilt for the untidy house. Guilt for not being the perfect, smiling, ever-capable mother and wife.

And guilt for daring to want something for herself.

Because even now, even in 2025, a woman prioritising her own joy is still seen as radical.

How dare she?

How dare she choose rest over responsibility, pleasure over productivity, self over service?

Multiply that scenario by a hundred. By a thousand. By a lifetime.

Every unspoken expectation, every invisible labour, every withheld truth.

Until one day, she stops resisting.

She gives up, and she surrenders to the script.

And that, my darling, is the real tragedy.

Because when women stop choosing themselves, their world dims.

We lose our spark. Our curiosity. Our humour. Our sensuality. Our sense of wonder.

We become functional, efficient, capable, impressive even, but hollow.

We call it balance, and we call it coping. When someone asks, we are fine.

But really, we're just surviving the story we were never meant to live.

Sacrifice becomes normal. And by sacrifice, I do not mean the poetic, heroic kind. I mean the quiet, daily erosion of self, the slow, steady disappearance of joy, ease, and freedom. All in the name of being good.

So, let me ask again: whose story are you living?

What sacrifices are you making?

And are you happy with them?

If your answer is yes, truly, deeply yes, then I am genuinely happy for you.

That is the whole point of this book. This book is not about shaming anyone for wanting the white picket fence or the diamond ring. It is about questioning whether you wanted it, or whether the world told you to.

This space is judgement-free. A space for curiosity, for truth-telling, for women to design lives that feel authentic, joyful, and deeply their own.

Fuck the Fairytale: Find Your Own Magic

So, is your story your own?

Or is it a mosaic of expectations and borrowed dreams?

The 'I shoulds.'

The 'good-girl' programming.

The cultural conditioning. The social media comparison trap. The patriarchy. The guilt. The endless striving for approval.

And what would your story look like if you had a blank page, no rules, no expectations, no audience?

What if, for once, you wrote it just for you? Would you still choose the same things? Would you still live in the same place, do the same work, love the same way? Would you still keep apologising for your needs?

Food for thought.

Breaking free of the fairytale trap isn't about rejecting love, or beauty, or hope. It is about reclaiming *you*.

The *you* who existed before you learned to shrink. The *you* who used to dream wildly, laugh loudly, and feel everything.

It's about rewriting what happily ever after means, not as an ending, but as a beginning.

It's about saying:

'I don't need to be rescued. I am perfectly capable of saving myself.'

'I don't want the fairytale. I want what feels like the truth.'

'I don't need a crown or a castle; I need peace.'

'I don't need a magic wand. I am the magic.'

And maybe that is the real revolution. Women no longer waiting for permission to live fully, loudly, unapologetically.

Because here's the thing: when you start designing a life that lights you up, everything else begins to shift.

The guilt quiets. The resentment fades. The sparkle comes back.

You stop asking, "Is this enough?" and start saying, "This feels right."

You start making decisions not from fear or duty, but from alignment.

And when you do that, when you begin to write your own story, the world around you will resist at first.

It always does. But stay the course. I implore you, my darling girl.

Because on the other side of that resistance is freedom.

Not the shiny kind you can photograph, but the quiet kind, the kind that settles into your bones.

That freedom is the beginning of your real story, my darling. The story where you wake up, stretch your wings, and remember that you were never meant to be the princess waiting in the tower. You were meant to be the woman who built her own damn kingdom.

So, let's begin.

Find Your Own Magic: A Guided Reflection

We have spent years living inside stories that weren't ours to begin with, stories written by family expectations, social rules, and invisible *shoulds*.

This reflection space is for you to use in whatever way you wish, and it might just be the first tiny step into breaking a spell that was cast on us all those years ago, when we were little girls playing with that Barbie Dreamhouse.

It is about rewriting your story, not to be the perfect fairytale, but to be really and truly yours.

The Story You Were Told

- What were the unspoken rules you grew up with about what a good woman, partner, mother, or professional should be?

- What did those rules teach you about success, love, or worth?

- Write them out, even the quiet ones that shaped you when no one was looking.

Mandy Merrifield

Sahar: The Story I Chose

Order.

That was the rhythm of the world I grew up in. Not a rhythm I chose, but one I stepped into out of necessity.

At just seven years old, after a tragic incident, I lost my father.

He was a merchant navy ship captain with a wide, worldly view, and with this sudden demise, our very world changed overnight.

What was once open and expansive became narrow and defined. My mother, a young widow, carried the weight of our lives with quiet courage. She didn't just raise me and my siblings; she protected us, anchored us, and taught us how to survive with dignity.

Growing up in that world, I was meant to be many things: a devoted daughter, a loving wife, a nurturing mother.

'Good' was the guiding word.

To be 'good' was to be secure. To be predictable was to be protected. So I did what was needed, I became the girl who didn't ask for too much, who excelled quietly, who made herself easy to love. I learned to survive by fitting in, by honouring the script, even when parts of me longed to speak a different language.

And for a time, that silence felt like safety.

The story was carefully crafted, wrapped in love and tradition, and passed down like an heirloom. And for a long time, I wore it with pride, and it served me well.

I was a diligent student, excelling in academics and extracurriculars; a responsible daughter; the girl who did what was expected of her.

I ticked every box: education, marriage, children, career. By every external measure, I was living the fairytale that had been written for me.

But deep down, something in me knew there had to be more. Not more in the sense of accumulation or out of dissatisfaction, more in the sense of *colour*.

Texture. Depth. Curiosity.

I wanted a life that wasn't just polished from the outside, but felt alive on the inside.

The truth is, my story didn't unravel in a single moment, nor was it a spectacular crash or a trauma-filled series of events. It wasn't the result of a disastrous, life-altering catastrophe where I woke up one day and decided to rebel against the script.

What I'm trying to say is this: it was a gentle unfolding.

It was slower, like threads loosening over time. I began to notice how certain parts of me were dimming. I could feel it most in the quiet moments, when I would find myself staring out the window, daydreaming of something I couldn't name.

And yet, life on paper was full and beautiful.

A public servant, working in policy and governance, grounded in purpose and structure. Married to a loving husband whose diplomatic career took us across continents and to places I could never have imagined. A mother of two vibrant teenagers.

I was genuinely grateful.

Yet beneath that gratitude, there was a quiet tug.

A soft, steady whisper suggesting that something more was waiting to be discovered, not because anything was missing in a dramatic sense, but because something within me longed to feel more fully expressed.

It started with small awakenings.

The first time I sat behind a radio microphone and felt more alive than I had in years.

The first time a stranger wrote to me, saying the outfit I had designed for them made them feel confident again.

The first time I styled a table for my food blog and realised I wasn't just setting dinner, I was creating art.

These were not grand acts of rebellion.

They were breadcrumbs, leading me back to myself.

I began to realise that while the fairytale was good, in my case, it was simply unfinished.

The version I was handed prized predictability and sacrifice.

The version I wanted celebrated creativity, independence, and authenticity.

And so, I began to rewrite.

My story, as it turns out, is not about rejecting the old fairytale, it is about tailoring it to fit.

My fairytale includes love, family, and meaningful work.

It also includes self-expression, freedom, and a voice that is fully my own. It's not about choosing between tradition and ambition; it's about weaving them together until they feel seamless.

That is where the magic lives: in the blending, not the breaking.

Still, the expectations don't disappear just because you see them clearly.

I catch myself sometimes, the quiet pressure to be endlessly accommodating, to have everything polished and perfect, to hold the façade of being effortlessly capable.

These invisible standards show up in the way I hesitate before saying no, or feel guilty for choosing rest over productivity.

The old voices, the ones that tell me 'you *should* be doing more,' still visit.

But I know how to quiet them now.

I step into my kitchen, tie my hair back, and cook something spontaneous. I leave the dishes until morning. I turn on music, dance barefoot, and laugh with my husband and kids about how ridiculous life can be.

I remind myself that being human is messy, and that's okay.

Those small rebellions, choosing joy, choosing imperfection, choosing *me*, are where my freedom lies.

Love

Growing up, I was taught that a good woman loved deeply, gave generously, and asked for little in return. She found fulfilment in the giving itself.

I carried that teaching like an invisible script, believing that love was about accommodation.

I held back my needs, thinking it was noble.

I waited to be understood instead of speaking up.

I wore patience like armour.

But over time, I realised that love doesn't read minds, it listens to truth.

Now I know that love is not about shrinking or staying silent.

Love is not about fitting into someone else's story at the expense of your own.

Real love makes room.

Real love celebrates your voice instead of fearing it.

Real love lets you breathe without asking for permission.

When I began speaking up, using *my* voice, honestly, vulnerably, and unapologetically, something truly beautiful happened.

Love rose to meet me there.

My marriage deepened as I allowed myself to be fully seen.

Mandy Merrifield

Relationships

Friendships that looked just right from the outside, I've known those well. The ones steeped in shared laughter, inside jokes, and years of memories. They felt safe, familiar, and full of history.

When the time came to let go of some of those connections, it wasn't about conflict, it was about growth.

There comes a point when you realise that some relationships thrive in a version of you that no longer exists.

And that's okay.

You can love people deeply and still outgrow them.

When those stories began to fade, it didn't feel like loss; it felt like turning the page.

The friendships that remain, the ones that have evolved with me, are rooted in honesty and ease. These are the people who see me clearly.

And these friendships, these people, are the ones I hold close.

My definition of love has softened and expanded as I've grown.

It's no longer just about romance or family, it's about how I meet myself.

Loving myself now means giving space to my curiosity, honouring my rest, and creating simply because I can.

Loving myself means celebrating small wins, forgiving the little stumbles, and trusting that I am always a work in progress, and that is enough.

Money

Money and success are two words that once carried more weight than they should have. I was raised to believe security came first, passion later.

Stability was the prize, and ambition was something you managed carefully so it did not tip the balance.

For a long time, I followed that rulebook.

But life has a way of nudging you towards your truth. Somewhere along the way, I came to understand that money is not just the number on a payslip; it is the energy of impact, of showing up and adding value.

Success, for me, is not about hierarchy; it is about alignment.

Along the way, I have made choices that defy the conventional narrative.

Stepping back from my career to raise my children is a perfect example. On paper, it looked like a detour, but in my heart, it felt like alignment.

I was choosing presence over performance.

It was both daunting and freeing, all at once.

Another time I stepped away was to join my husband on his diplomatic posting overseas: a chapter filled with adventure, learning, and connection.

It wasn't a pause in purpose; it was a beautiful redirection.

My journey did not slow down because of those choices. Those choices expanded it, adding depth, perspective, and experiences that no résumé could ever fully reflect.

They led to vibrant seasons of growth, both personal and shared.

The time at home taught me lessons no office ever could: patience, adaptability, empathy, and an entirely new understanding of leadership.

Each time I re-entered the workforce, I did so with a richer, wiser perspective. Ironically, I climbed faster than I ever had before. Because I wasn't chasing validation anymore, I was grounded in purpose.

Now, I define success as living in alignment with my values.

Titles and applause no longer motivate me.

Motivation comes from integrity, from knowing within myself that I am doing work that reflects who I am, what matters to me, and making a difference by adding value. My career is no longer about the day-to-day tasks, accolades, or professional recognition, nor about the figure in my bank account each month. It is about creating impact that lasts.

I no longer chase the illusion of having it all.

I have learned that having it all does not mean doing it all. It means choosing what matters and doing that well.

Self

My relationship with my body has been one of quiet evolution.

I have always been fairly comfortable in my skin, but that does not mean I was immune to the subtle messages about how a woman should look, move, or age. The expectations were never shouted; they were the quiet, implied subtext of compliments, delivered through mainstream media, where effortless perfection was put on a pedestal, even though that perfection was anything but effortless.

A few years ago, my body demanded my attention.

Health challenges brought me face-to-face with my own fragility: adult acne, hair loss, and an acute episode of septic arthritis. These moments were humbling, but also clarifying.

Fuck the Fairytale: Find Your Own Magic

In my mid-thirties, I found myself battling acne I had never experienced, even as a teenager. It lingered for a few years, unexpected and relentless.

At first, I told myself I would feel better once it cleared. But as the months stretched on, I realised something important: I couldn't keep postponing my happiness.

Because who can say what comes next? Hair fall, greying strands, other health concerns, there is always going to be something. Waiting for perfect skin or perfect hair to feel good meant postponing joy. I didn't want to live like that anymore.

The shift came when I understood that happiness wasn't a few months away. It was already here, in the way I chose to see myself.

Acceptance and gratitude had to come first, not as a reward for results, but as the soil from which healing could grow. And that changed everything.

Over time, I started opting out.

I stopped consuming sugar and ultra-processed foods, stopped straightening my curly hair, and stopped the colouring routine that had become like Groundhog Day, simply leaving it as its natural black. I traded foundation for fresh skin, even while my acne was still healing, scars still visible.

I didn't stop covering up because everything had cleared.

I chose to show up as I was, not as I wished to be.

That decision wasn't about my skin; it was about self-respect. About trusting that confidence doesn't come from coverage, but from compassion.

I stopped apologising for how I looked on days I wasn't camera-ready, and it felt less like rebellion and more like a homecoming.

What you eat, what you think, who you surround yourself with, it all becomes part of your inner ecosystem.

Now, I care for my body as an act of gratitude, not control.

I eat clean because it feels good, not because I am chasing a shape.

I rest because it is necessary, not indulgent.

I move because it connects me to life, not because it burns calories.

Reclaiming my body hasn't been a battle; it has been a slow, joyful return to myself.

Family

Family expectations shaped me, but they never trapped me. I was fortunate to grow up in a home that valued kindness, achievement, and grace, but I also knew early on that I was wired a little differently.

I wanted to explore, to question, to blend tradition with imagination.

There were moments of quiet negotiation, times when my choices didn't fit the conventional mould.

But I never felt estranged from my roots.

Instead, I learned to hold both truths: I could honour where I came from while also walking a path uniquely mine.

Living differently doesn't mean rejection; it means expansion.

My life now is proof that you can love your heritage and evolve with it, with confidence, poise, and grace.

The community I have built, through work, creativity, and global connections from our time abroad, feels like a beautiful extended family. These relationships aren't bound by geography or tradition. They are built on mutual respect, shared curiosity, and the joy of being seen.

When you've lived across continents as I have, you realise that home is not a place; it is a feeling.

For me, home is the table filled with laughter, the conversations that flow without judgement, the people who let you be messy and marvellous all at once.

Faith

Faith and spirituality were constant companions in my upbringing, shaping what I valued, how I behaved, and what I aspired to. They taught me humility, service, and self-discipline.

These are the values that still anchor me today.

As I grew, I gently carved out space for my own understanding of faith, one that welcomed curiosity, honoured individuality, and embraced emotional depth.

Religion and spirituality became less about following rules blindly, and more about cultivating a living, breathing connection with meaning itself.

Now, I find the sacred in the everyday: in the ritual of meditation, in the rhythm of cooking, in the discipline that keeps my dreams from drifting. I find divinity in creativity, in generosity, in laughter shared after a long day.

Magic, for me, isn't mystical or far away.

Magic is what happens when intention meets alignment.

Magic is the quiet synchronicity of people, opportunities, and moments showing up just when you are ready for them.

Magic is the sense that life is conspiring with you, not against you, if only you are paying attention.

Lessons

There was a time when I believed stability and freedom were opposites.

To be responsible, I had to be restrained.

To be grounded, I had to stay within the lines.

But somewhere between continents, raising children, building careers, and rediscovering myself, I realised that freedom isn't the absence of structure.

Freedom is the presence of truth.

My 9 to 5 grounds me in service.

My creative projects set me free.

Service and creativity feed the other: one anchors, the other uplifts. I am not living a double life; I am living a layered one.

The fairytale I was told had me believe life should follow a sequence: education, marriage, family, work, stability. But the story I have chosen allows for expansion. It allows for detours, curiosity, and reinvention.

And maybe that is the real fairytale, not the one where everything goes according to plan, but the one where you learn to dance with change.

Happiness, for me, isn't about grand achievements.

Happiness is in the everyday, in the gentle rhythm of a life lived with awareness.

Happiness is in my children's laughter, in the stories I tell on the radio, in the outfits I design that make someone stand taller, and in a meal that turns into a memory.

Happiness is in showing up as I am, without needing to impress or apologise.

I am happiest when I know I am contributing something real: a spark of inspiration, a sense of connection, and a reminder that we all have the right to live our own version of 'enough'.

A love letter to my younger self

Dear Sahar,

If I could write to my fifteen-year-old self, I'd tell her this:

You are a firecracker of ideas and heart, and that is your magic.

Don't dim it to make others comfortable.

The world will ask you to shrink, to stay within the lines.

Don't.

Life will take you across continents, through languages, roles, and seasons. You will be many things: a public servant, a content creator, a mother, a storyteller, and you will weave them all into one life that is uniquely yours.

You will stumble.

You will face health scares, and heartbreaks, and self-doubt.

You will rise, stronger, wiser, shinier.

Keep chasing flavour, not perfection.

Keep choosing curiosity over fear.

And know this: the fairytale was never about the castle, the prince, or the perfect ending.

It was always about the woman who learned to write her own story.

And the best part? The fairytale doesn't end; it simply becomes yours to continue, in every choice you make, every truth you embrace, and every page you write.

And you, Sahar, are doing just that.

Chapter 3:
Choose Joy

Joy isn't a mood.

It's not a permanent high, or the curated version of happiness you see on someone's Instagram grid.

Joy is quieter.

Truer.

It is that moment of exhale when you finally stop performing and actually land in your own life.

Fairytales sell us the idea that joy is something that is earned, a reward for getting it right, for doing the right thing, for working hard and ticking all of the boxes.

The degree.

The job.

The body.

The relationship.

The mortgage.

If you do all of these things, and even better, if you do them in the right order, joy will supposedly arrive on the doorstep of that massively mortgaged house like a charmingly wrapped parcel, just waiting for you to collect it.

Except, we know that doesn't happen.

We are always waiting for joy, waiting for the next milestone, the next achievement, the next thing to make it all feel worth it. We live in a culture that worships progress and productivity, where slowing down looks suspicious, and contentment feels like laziness. We keep moving, keep doing, keep chasing the next thing because that is where we have been told that happiness lives.

But joy isn't actually found at the top of a checklist where all the boxes have been ticked. It doesn't arrive with fanfare or fireworks. It appears quietly, unexpectedly, in the small moments, the unplanned happenings, the honest, real, funny, and perfectly ordinary parts of life that unfold when you're too tired or too honest to pretend anymore.

Joy comes when you (and I know this is going to sound corny) stop and smell the roses.

It shows up when you are present, when you are here in your own life, rather than running the endless treadmill of what's next.

For me, it is when I watch my beloved pooch snoring away on the satin pillow next to me. It is when I am coaching a client, and I see the exact moment a light bulb flickers in her eyes, that spark of self-awareness that changes everything. It is when I see my daughter curled up on my sofa, cup of tea in her favourite mug, in her pyjamas mid-morning, safe and content.

These are the things that make me content.

Once upon a time, I used to think it was the big house, the incredible career, the holidays, and the Manolos. I used to believe these glittering, hedonistic trappings were what happiness was. That these things would somehow anchor me in joy, make me enough, prove that I had made it.

How wrong I was.

It wasn't until everything was stripped away, until I was standing in the rubble of my own life with nothing left to perform, nothing left to prove, that I understood where my happiness truly lived. It wasn't in the striving. It wasn't in the 'shoulds.' It was in the small, quiet things that didn't need to be posted, polished, or performed.

And that's the problem.

Most of us, myself included for many years, don't know how to stop long enough to notice the small things. We are far too busy chasing what joy should look like.

Once upon a time, a little girl learned a word that would quietly run her whole life.

Should.

She *should* be polite.

She *should* smile.

She *should* share.

She *should* help.

She *should* not be too loud, too demanding, too emotional, too much.

Should becomes the invisible text in the fairytale, the one that dictates what good looks like.

Good daughter.

Good partner.

Good mother.

Good employee.

Good woman.

It is subtle at first. It sounds harmless, even virtuous.

You don't realise how early it starts shaping you. You learn to swallow your opinions to keep the peace. You learn to say yes even when your whole body screams no.

You learn to soften yourself, to shrink a little, to take up less space, because good girls don't rock the boat.

But where does 'should' come from?

It doesn't come from your heart, my darling.

It comes from conditioning, from generations of stories that taught women that compliance equals worthiness. That sacrifice equals love. That silence equals grace.

Fuck the Fairytale: Find Your Own Magic

It comes from centuries of stories about women who were rewarded for being good, for cleaning the floors, for waiting quietly, for forgiving endlessly, for staying small.

'Should' is Cinderella scrubbing the floor because being chosen is the ultimate goal.

It is Sleeping Beauty waiting in suspended animation until someone else decides she's worthy of being woken up.

It is every woman who has ever smiled through exhaustion because she was told that being needed is the same as being loved.

Living by the 'shoulds' is like living with a quiet thief. It steals your voice, your instincts, your joy, piece by piece. It convinces you that peace means pleasing everyone but yourself.

Have you ever said yes when deep down, in the pit of your stomach, you wanted so badly to say no? Have you ever felt that tightening in your chest when your own needs are pushed to the side, again, because someone else's comfort matters more?

And what about that resentment that builds over time? That quiet, gnawing ache that comes from being the one who always shows up for others, while no one seems to notice that you are running on empty?

What about that bone-deep, mind-shattering exhaustion that no amount of sleep can fix, because it's not actually your body that's tired. It's your soul.

That's what living by 'should' does.

It keeps you stuck in a story where your worth is tied to what you give, how much you endure, and how well you perform. It is constant self-abandonment dressed up as the right thing to do.

Should is slowly destroying you.

But here's the thing about joy; she waits patiently. She doesn't leave you, even when you forget her. She sits silently beneath the noise, beneath the performance, beneath the 'shoulds', waiting for you to remember her again.

She's there in the moments you stop running. When you finally exhale. When you choose presence over perfection.

Joy doesn't need you to have it all figured out. She doesn't ask for proof or performance. She doesn't live in the future you're chasing or the past you regret.

She lives here, in this moment, in the softness of now.

Maybe joy isn't something we need to find, but something we need to remember.

Maybe she's been here all along, patiently whispering beneath the noise: You're allowed to stop. You're allowed to feel. You're allowed to be.

Because when you stop living for the 'shoulds', something beautiful happens. The world doesn't collapse. The sky doesn't fall in. What happens instead is quiet, peaceful, revolutionary.

You begin to feel again.

You begin to notice again.

You begin to live again.

Joy is the deep inhale after years of holding your breath.

It's the laughter that bubbles up unexpectedly when you stop trying to control everything.

It's the peace that comes when you finally understand that your worth was never something to earn.

Joy isn't a mood.

It is a homecoming.

Find Your Own Magic: A Guided Reflection

Before you turn the page, pause.

This is where you get to stop performing, stop pleasing for the sake of it, and start listening to the quiet truths beneath all the 'shoulds' that have shaped your choices so far.

The Story You've Been Living

- When you look at your current life, where do you notice you're still following those old scripts?

- Where do you catch yourself saying "I should…" instead of "I want to…"?

- What parts of your life feel scripted, on autopilot, performative, people-pleasing, or heavy?

Angela: The Right to Be Here

I never quite know how to answer the question, "Who are you now?"

I suppose the simplest truth is this: I am a work in progress, getting stronger every day.

I am lucky, happy, scarred in places that don't show, but yet those scars influence everything.

I love my babies, and their babies, fiercely. I love my husband, my friends, and people who care about fairness.

My sense of social justice has always lived right under my skin, maybe because I know how it feels to be unseen, unprotected, and told that my worth is conditional.

I am still learning. But I am here, standing strong, heart open.

This is me now.

Being the Good Girl

I grew up believing that being a good girl was my job.

Before my dad died, I was six then, an only child, I remember feeling safe while performing goodness. After he died, being the good girl felt like survival. I needed to keep Mum happy. Her approval was oxygen; her disapproval was a storm that could tear the walls down.

She taught me that a woman's ultimate success was getting a man to marry you.

The quality of the man? Not discussed.

His ability to love? Irrelevant.

Just get one.

Keep him.

Be grateful.

And my family? Well, we were the outsiders.

'They' were the rich, educated, rule-makers.

'We' were the downtrodden victims who should work the system and never expect more.

That mindset was suffocating. But it was all I knew.

So yes, I bought the idea that the only fairytale I could expect was getting a man to marry me.

I believed a boy liking me was worth more than anything I might be.

The Breaking of the World

The day of my father's wake is tattooed on my insides. I was told by a cousin not to be sad about his death because he wasn't really my dad. I ran to Mum and Nan, terrified, and they confirmed it.

I was adopted.

Everything shifted.

My grief became… inconvenient.

I learned that my sadness upset others.

I learned to swallow my needs whole. I learned that a child could be given away, and that the child in question was then lucky when someone else wanted it.

It was at this juncture in my world that rejection became the defining weapon, the bomb, the ultimate felling blow that I would forever and a day strive to avoid in all circumstances.

Mum would later weaponise my adoption papers, pulling them out during drinking rants: "When your father died, I could have put you back in the home." She was implying two things: he was the one who wanted me, not her, and that a widow would be justified in giving back a child who wasn't biologically hers.

Imagine being six years old.

Grieving.

Then, learning you were someone's mistake, only tolerated out of convenience.

You don't know the language for trauma at six.

But your nervous system learns it fluently.

That was the moment I stopped being seen.

Pretty

My mother's life revolved around men, drinking with them, chasing them, placing them above everything else, including me. I saw and heard things I should not have. When I cried or felt uncomfortable, suddenly I was selfish, because I was trying to stop Mummy from having friends.

So I learned that men are the priority.

And I learned that children, especially adopted ones, come last.

I wasn't a pretty child at all, but as I grew up and that changed, I learned that my beauty was my only real currency.

Mum rarely praised me for anything but how pretty I was.

So I made pretty work for me… even though it felt like walking around in an outfit two sizes too small, outwardly admired, inwardly trapped.

And later, when relationships with men hurt me, Mum's advice was: "If you want to keep a man, you have to put up with that."

And then there was the infamous benchmark that defined my standards: "He doesn't knock you about or gamble."

As if that was the measure of being loved.

I internalised a very low bar and spent decades tripping over it.

There was one place I rebelled: education.

I craved knowledge. Hunger is not a strong enough word.

A scholarship took me into a private school filled with the type of people my family resented: wealthy, educated, and travelled. The 'they' I was taught to fear. Yet those were the people who showed me that I was smart.

They also showed me I absolutely did not belong in their sphere.

It was acceptable to be the token scholarship girl. It was not acceptable to be friends with their children.

But I was capable. A mind worth investing in.

And while school woke my intellect, there was still nothing that could shake the belief that being chosen by a man was the ultimate prize.

So, I existed in two conflicting truths: I wanted to know more and be part of this educated world I had landed in (truth be told: I never thought that I would be brilliant), and then, I needed to be wanted.

Being wanted is the opposite of rejection. This applied to friendships as well.

Brilliance always dimmed its light; being wanted won every time.

Hypervigilance

This is a word I now understand.

Growing up with alcoholism means you learn to scan every room, every breath of mood change. It becomes cellular, a readiness to flee, to appease, to shrink.

When I married my first husband, a good man, truly, honestly, I thought I had won.

A steady man.

A respectable man.

A man without a drinking problem.

What more could I possibly deserve?

I never asked whether we were good for each other. I just felt lucky he wanted me.

And that gratitude for being chosen?

It gave me friendships that were based on not being rejected, rather than shared values, boundaries, and dignity. Friendships that lasted far too many years, and wasted far too much of my time.

I stayed in a relationship with crumbs and called myself fortunate to eat.

He worked constantly. He succeeded. He was respected.

I felt like an assistant in my own marriage.

Lonely in a shared home.

But every time I voiced my loneliness, loudly and angrily, guilt screamed louder:

'He doesn't hit you.'

'He works hard.'

'You aren't bringing in money. Why should you want more?'

I learned to believe I was: too loud.

Too emotional. Too needy. Too much.

And somehow, all at once: not enough.

When intimacy faded, except for making babies, it struck right at the core of the only worth I had been taught I possessed. If beauty was value, and beauty was not wanted… who was I then?

I wasn't taught partnership. I was taught possession.

Keep the man.

Don't upset him; he doesn't deserve your anger and discontent.

You are lucky to have him.

But my inner voice kept whispering: "This can't be all there is."

It would take years to listen, because I was so scared of being rejected again.

But healing isn't a revelation.

Healing is repetition. Choosing, every day, to rewrite the script you were handed.

Learning

It started quietly.

A single class.

A single assignment.

A single lecturer telling me that my thinking mattered, not my appearance, not my compliance.

My mind.

Safety in education has always made sense to me. It was the first place I learned I was worth more than what I could offer men. When I began the study journey, it was like coming home to a version of myself I had left behind decades ago, the girl hungry to learn, the girl who lit up when she felt smart, the girl who didn't need to be looked at to be seen.

 Juggling kids, marriage and study should have exhausted me.

Instead, it energised me.

I wasn't chasing a grade; I was chasing freedom.

Every essay, every late-night reading session told me: 'You are more than pretty. You always were.'

And quietly, without making a scene, a woman was forming who did not need to be chosen to feel worthy.

There came a point when the walls of my marriage felt too tight. Not because he was a bad man, but because I had outgrown the shape of the life we built together.

The end of my marriage was dramatic because it was the rejection I had always been so fearful of. It didn't matter that neither of us was happy. It mattered that yet another person who told me they loved me felt that I was disposable.

Mandy Merrifield

It was devastating.

When my husband left me, vulnerability crashed over me like a tidal wave. I finally had the education I had fought for, but financially, I was naïve. I had no idea what our money situation was.

None.

As an only child living away from my hometown, I did not have family rallying around me as many people do in times of crisis. I had no one to turn to. I was my own safety net, and I knew without any shadow of a doubt that I was alone.

And suddenly, I had to protect myself in the middle of emotional collapse. I had to find a lawyer. I had to make decisions I had never been allowed to make.

As I tried to care for my children, one of whom was very ill, I was also facing the biggest fear of my life, that rejected, alone, discarded feeling.

I was not the one who chose to exit my marriage, and there were consequences to being the one who had been left.

There was judgement, whispers, and the shame women are taught to swallow.

But you do not need permission to save your own life.

And I learned: Never again will I allow myself to be unseen or taken for granted, and I will never be financially dependent or blind again.

Now, today, my financial independence is non-negotiable.

The respect in my current marriage means those boundaries are met with understanding, not resentment.

I have been able to help my children buy homes because I would much rather see them thrive now than wait for an inheritance.

I want to travel, to age with dignity, and never become a burden on anyone.

Mistakes have been made.

Lessons have been learned.

And I am not done learning.

Forgiveness

People imagine forgiveness as softness, turning the other cheek, letting it all go.

But in my life, forgiveness has been the most ferocious thing I have ever done. Having acknowledged that, I will admit that there is still some forgiving to do.

I forgave my mother for the traumas she passed down, not because they were okay, but because she was broken long before I was born.

I forgave the little girl inside her who never had a chance to heal.

I forgave the family narratives that told me my worth was conditional.

I forgave the men who only ever saw the pretty surface, even when my insides were burning to be truly seen and known.

And I forgave myself.

For not knowing sooner.

For loving too small.

For having believed I was lucky just to be tolerated.

For trusting too blindly.

Forgiveness didn't clean my past; it cleared my path for the future.

Motherhood: My First Real Love

I worked my way through the hardest parts of my life, fuelled by love.

Not romantic love.

No, that has always been too fragile, too conditional.

But the fierce, immovable love I have for my precious and magnificent babies.

Mandy Merrifield

I have always been a good mum.

Even at my lowest, I loved well.

My three babies saved me in ways they will never fully understand.

They gave me a purpose bigger than survival.

They are my motivation, and they are my joy.

I made sure they always knew how prayed for, planned and wished for they were, and still are. I never wanted them to doubt for even a nanosecond how loved they are.

That has been my mission: my children know their worth.

Looking at my daughter now, the truly outstanding mother she is, I know my message has been passed on. She knows the privilege, not the right, of loving a child.

My children forced me to imagine a future worth living in.

And they expanded my heart into rooms I didn't know existed.

I learned tenderness from being what I needed as a child: present, protective, patient.

I gave them the stability I never had.

I gave them the truth that love doesn't need to be earned.

And when grandchildren arrived, beautiful, cheeky little souls, I discovered joy that arrives without conditions.

My love has multiplied across generations.

A legacy of care where fear once ruled.

Motherhood across generations

At first, my mum criticised my parenting. I think she felt replaced, almost as if I had taken her role as the most important person in my life away from her.

Fuck the Fairytale: Find Your Own Magic

Motherhood lit a fire in me that I had never managed to ignite for myself. No one and nothing was going to distract me from being the mum my babies needed.

And as my children grew, so did I.

That strength, the kind you develop when you realise little hearts depend on you, spilled into all other parts of my life, especially education.

To her credit, my mum softened.

She grew into a woman capable of loving my children in ways she never knew how to love me. Watching her become someone gentler healed places in me that had once felt unfixable.

When she died, I had already done the work, already forgiven, already reached that point where love replaced the pain.

I miss my mum every single day, and I love the woman she managed to become.

Family is complicated

Holding love for family while creating a life that looks nothing like theirs… that is one of my longest arc storylines, and certainly, it is a lesson that never ends.

When I broke away from my adoptive family in 1983, I gained the freedom to become whoever I wanted. And, strangely enough, now that time has aged us and the generation with the drinking problem has passed on, we get on well. Most of us decided early not to continue the cycle, and the absence of chaos has left room for closeness.

But my biological family?

That has been something else entirely.

Years ago, in 1991, I met my biological mother and elder sister, the child who had been kept.

What followed was love-bombing, big promises, and then the familiar sting of invisibility. I was invited to a major family event and once I arrived… I was no one.

Not mentioned. Not introduced. Not acknowledged.

When I asked why, she said, "I didn't know who to say you were."

That wound cut deep. It was an enormous rejection, one that I accepted without question, and one that I internalised right in my core.

But the sharper pain?

My husband (the first one) and adoptive mother were angry at me for even going, offering no sympathy, no comfort.

The message was clear: How you feel and what you want doesn't matter. Don't upset anyone.

It took years, decades in fact, to undo that belief.

Now, I hold my ground.

I insist on being treated with respect.

And that is uncomfortable for them, the biologicals.

They want me to be grateful just to be tolerated. They expect admiration for their generosity in acknowledging me at all. And when I call out that behaviour, they disappear.

For years at a time.

But now? I do not take it personally.

I know my worth.

I will not beg to belong.

I will never again allow someone to make me feel like a visitor in my own life.

Being known, still yet a secret

My biological father was happy to know me privately, but publicly? Absolutely not.

He wanted me to visit, but I had to pretend to be a friend. I told him plainly that I would not be hidden and that if we connected on Ancestry, I would be honest with any matches that emerged.

That forced his hand.

Today, the interactions with my biological father are careful, considerate, and mutually respectful.

Some of his children, my half-siblings, accept me.

Some do not.

I do not share my children with anyone who shows up without love and integrity. My babies did not choose the complicated history that has come before them, and I will protect them fiercely until, and unless, they themselves decide otherwise.

A Beautiful Life

Theoretically, I was raised as a Catholic, although I wouldn't label myself as a Christian now.

At least not in the organised religion sense.

However, I deeply believe: how we treat people reflects our own worth, not theirs.

That belief took me into NGO work, volunteer work, and advocacy. I care about strong public welfare, healthcare, education, and the systems that keep people from falling through cracks I know all too well.

Do I struggle with having a beautiful life now, with travel and joy, while knowing what that same money could mean for charity?

Yes.

It is a delicate balance, and I am constantly learning.

Mandy Merrifield

My Magic

Magic isn't found in escape or fantasy for me.

Magic is flesh and blood.

Magic has my grandchildren's faces.

There is a wonder that comes with knowing, as an adopted person, that when I carried my daughter, her eggs were already inside her. Which means her children were, in part, carried inside me too.

I didn't come from anyone.

But now?

I have babies who have babies who come from me.

I could cry just writing that.

It is the greatest privilege of my life.

I travel for months each year, with the intention that I'm not overly intrusive.

But those babies, biological and step-grandbabies, they are the moon and the stars to me.

Just Me

In 2017, heartbreak struck.

I was hurt deeply by someone very close to me.

And I knew, as that pain hit, that I was in danger.

I could feel the pull: slipping into old coping mechanisms; fear that I would, like my mother, start drinking, isolate myself from the world, watch television around the clock, eat chocolate and swallow tranquilisers. Numbing myself into nothingness.

I recognised I was at a crossroads. The pain was constant.

So I left.

I left my grown children, my relationship, my entire life. I spent seven months travelling alone in Europe.

No one's mum.

No one's daughter.

No one's partner.

No one's ex.

Just me.

Alone, without language, and without certainty, I found joy.

Fear.

Friendship.

Music.

I joined choirs. I walked unfamiliar streets. I laughed with strangers who became friends.

And the greatest revelation?

I was enough.

People were kind to me because of who they saw, not because they had to be. Their behaviour reflected their character, not my worth.

Was it late in my life to learn this lesson? Maybe.

But not too late.

Love, Redefined

I didn't expect to find love again.

Not the safe, warm, equal kind.

Not the kind that sees all of me, the scars, the strength, the silliness, and says: I'll take it. All of it.

But I did.

This love isn't about possession.

It is about partnership.

No pedestal.

No silent suffering.

No shrinking to fit.

I love my husband because he adds to my life, not because he completes it.

That difference is everything.

Today

I do have regrets.

I wish I had a career that marked my place in the world more publicly, something impactful, something financially empowering. I admire women who manage both great love and successful careers.

But I also know this: the healthy years my husband and I have left are a gift.

We are choosing to spend them together: living, adventuring, laughing.

He is my best friend. My life is richer with him in it.

He does not complete my life; that is not his role. He very simply, beautifully enhances it.

My children are good people, the kind of humans I would choose as friends. We have navigated challenges, serious health issues, storms that could have swallowed us… and we are still standing.

I have a small circle of real friends. The ones who remain are gold, the ones who stayed once I stopped being grateful for simply being included.

A Safe Place

Growing up, safety was unpredictable.

Fuck the Fairytale: Find Your Own Magic

I learned to read every room before I walked into it.

To make myself agreeable.

Invisible.

Convenient.

Hypervigilance is a habit born from survival, and it doesn't settle easily.

So becoming my own safe place was a practice: cooking myself dinner even when I was eating alone. Speaking kindly to myself in the mirror. Opening mail instead of fearing what is inside the envelope. Wearing clothes because I liked them. Resting without guilt. Celebrating without permission.

I filled my space with calm.

I made my home reflect me, not who I was trying to please.

One night, alone in the home I had created, I realised: I wasn't lonely.

I was safe.

And that may be the greatest plot twist of my life.

I still like feeling pretty.

I enjoy it.

But the difference now?

Pretty is not the point.

I am beautiful because I am:

Brave.

Educated.

Funny.

Capable.

Empathetic.

A devoted mum.

Mandy Merrifield

A fiercely proud Nonna.

A woman who keeps rising, and who finds joy in every day.

Pretty is just a single brushstroke on a very large canvas.

I no longer live by the story I was born into.

I write my own.

Every day I choose: Truth over performance. Boundaries over appeasement. Joy over justification. Curiosity over fear.

And I choose connections that deepen my life, not drain it.

I didn't get the fairytale.

I was never promised a white knight. I did not deserve one.

But you know what? I got better than I was told to hope for or expect.

I got a life where I belong to myself.

A family built on love, not fear.

A partner who meets me eye to eye.

A voice strong enough to speak its truth.

And a heart that knows it's worth.

Finally.

And somewhere along the way, I stopped trying to be the princess and became the author.

I stopped being grateful for crumbs and started baking my own damn bread.

I have always had to fend for myself, but now I realise I can rely on others, the ones I have chosen from my healthy place, and I know now, I am the hero of my story.

I always was.

My happy ending isn't a wedding.

Or a man's approval.

Or beauty that gets noticed.

My happy ending is this: I am living a life I choose.

A life I built.

A life where my children and grandbabies will inherit strength instead of fear.

I am a full-grown woman who knows her value and takes up her space, without apology.

That, right there, is the real magic.

And it was in me the whole time.

A love letter to my younger self

Dear Angela,

Darling, precious girl.

You are truly wonderful.

Your heart is kind. Your mind is sharp. Your worth is undoubted.

Please, please believe that you are worthy of your place in the world.

You are easy to love.

The people in your life are so very lucky to have you.

You don't have to feel grateful that anyone wants to be your friend, boyfriend or anything else.

How you came into this world and under what circumstances does not define you.

Be discerning.

Decide who is right to be in your life.

Don't wait to be chosen and feel grateful for it.

You choose.

You decide.

You know what you are worth and take nothing less, no matter what significant people in your life might tell you. These are their issues, not yours.

Don't rush into romantic relationships.

Give yourself the love and support to go into whichever field makes your heart truly soar.

The rest will come.

I promise.

Chapter 4:
The Waiting Game

2007-ish

Perfect house.

Happy, beautiful children.

Husband.

Convenient job.

Unhappy me.

What the fuck? Why?

I certainly couldn't work it out.

On the outside, I had everything a girl could want. The boxes were ticked, the milestones reached. I was the image of a life well-lived, the one that makes people nod approvingly at dinner parties and say, 'she's doing so well.' But on the inside, I was empty.

Not restless. Not even screaming. Just… nothing. Desolate.

And then came the guilt. So much guilt.

How dare I feel unfulfilled when I had everything? A husband who provided. Healthy children. A house with soft neutral tones and a mortgage we could manage. I should have been grateful. Right?

That is what I told myself. Over and over.

How could I think of walking away from that?

How could I break up a happy family?

What would happen to my girls?

Would I have enough money to live?

And the biggest question of all: what exactly was it that I did want?

I had no idea.

I only knew that something deep inside me, something ancient, intuitive, and wordless, was whispering that I couldn't keep living like this. But because I didn't know what to do, because the fear was bigger than the knowing, I did what women have been taught to do for centuries: I stayed still.

I stayed quiet.

I waited.

And waiting felt easier. Waiting was what was appropriate. Waiting was what the stories told us to do.

Because that's what the fairytales teach us.

That if you wait long enough, it will all work out in the end. That if you're good, patient, and kind, life will reward you. That if you keep going, if you swallow the ache and smooth the edges of your discomfort, eventually, someone or something will swoop in to make it all okay.

That is the lie we all inherited.

Let's think about Cinderella.

Cinderella: the woman who was taught to prove her worth through suffering, patience, and silence.

Sound familiar?

She was the ultimate good girl. She didn't rage. She didn't revolt. She endured. She scrubbed floors, smiled sweetly, and kept hoping that her goodness would one day be seen.

She waited for permission. She waited for love. She waited for validation. She waited for rescue.

That's the story we are fed. And it is dangerous.

Because it teaches women that the pathway to happiness isn't through our own power, but through being chosen.

Chosen for the job.

Chosen for the ring.

Fuck the Fairytale: Find Your Own Magic

Chosen for the house.

Chosen by someone else to finally be seen, worthy, enough.

The fairytale goes something like this: a sweet, humble girl keeps doing everything right, no complaints, no rebellion, until the universe rewards her. She is kind. She never gets angry. She never sets boundaries. She doesn't make waves. She just keeps believing.

And one day, because she is lucky, someone notices her goodness. They see how hard she has worked, how tirelessly she has held it all together, how loyal, patient, and forgiving she has been.

And then that person will save her.

Fabulous!

But is it?

This story is seductive because it sounds safe. Good things will come to those who wait.

Just as long as you don't demand more, disrupt the status quo, or question.

Therein lies the trap.

The fairytale isn't just a story; it's a script. And that script has been quietly running through our subconscious minds for decades.

As women, we internalised the idea that happiness is something to wait for.

We wait for approval. We wait for love. We wait for the right time, the right job, the right partner, the right body, the right moment to finally begin. We wait to start living until it all looks how it's supposed to.

And one of the biggest lies in all of this isn't just that happiness is promised, it's that it's promised after something.

After the proposal.

After the wedding.

After the kids.

Mandy Merrifield

After the mortgage is paid off.

After the promotion.

After retirement.

It's always after.

As if happiness lives somewhere out there, on the other side of effort and exhaustion and endurance. As if joy is a finish line you crawl toward, instead of something you're allowed to feel now, right in the middle of the mess.

But what happens in the meantime? What happens in the waiting?

Do we get to be happy while we are raising the kids, while the house is noisy and the dishes are still in the sink? Do we get to feel fulfilled before everything is perfectly aligned?

Do we get to breathe before the credits roll?

And what even is happiness?

Whoa! That's a big one. I don't think it's a question we are meant to answer quickly, so let's put it on a post-it for now.

Happiness is not a checkbox. It's not a photo-ready moment.

Happiness isn't a scene you arrive at. It is a rhythm, a pulse that sits underneath everything. But when you've been waiting your whole life for it to appear, it's hard to recognise the sound.

When you've built your life around other people's expectations, your parents, your partner, your friends, it is easy to forget what your own voice even sounds like.

The invisible 'they' of society silences us.

We stop asking questions like "What do I want?" and instead start asking "What should I want?"

And that is the difference between living a life and performing one.

Cinderella waited for someone to give her permission to leave her own story. And when she finally did, when the dress appeared and the ball beckoned, she still wasn't free. Because she didn't claim her freedom, it was handed to her.

She was chosen.

And then, just as quickly, she lost it again.

Midnight came. The magic faded. The slipper broke.

The story tells us that she is saved in the end, that the prince finds her, and she finally gets her reward. But what the story doesn't tell us is what happens after.

What happens when the glow fades, when she's back in the castle doing the emotional labour of a royal life she didn't design?

What happens when she looks around and realises that even in the happily-ever-after, she still doesn't feel at home in her own skin?

That was me.

The house, the kids, the husband, the job. It all looked perfect. But the feeling didn't match the picture.

And that's the thing no one tells you.

You can build the exact life you thought you wanted, the fairytale version with all the right pieces, and still feel like you're sleepwalking through your own story.

You can have everything and still ache for something more.

Even if you don't know what that 'more' is.

So maybe the rebellion isn't leaving everything behind, but waking up inside the life you already have and daring to ask, 'What if I wrote this differently?'

'What if I stopped waiting for permission?'

'What if I stopped hoping to be chosen?'

'What if I decided that I am already enough?' Not because I fit the story, but because I am finally writing my own?

Mandy Merrifield

Cleo:
The Story I Thought I Was Supposed to Live

Growing up, I didn't have the classic 'you need to be a good wife, find a husband, pop out two kids, keep the house tidy' messaging thrown at me.

My parents didn't push some outdated script.

If anything, it was the opposite.

I had amazing role models, and the biggest lessons were the simple ones: work hard, be a good person, look after your health, and build a life that feels like yours.

There was no pressure to follow a specific path.

No 'you should be a doctor', or 'make sure you marry well.'

I was given space to explore, to test things out, to figure out who I was.

And honestly, that's rare.

I can see now how lucky I was.

Even when you're carving out your own freedom, there's no escaping it completely. The fairytale finds a way to slip in anyway.

In my case, it was not from my parents, but from everywhere else.

It came through Disney movies, rom-coms, social media, magazines, and every story fed to young women about the way life goes if you're doing it right.

Even if no one sits you down to teach you this script, you absorb it.

The timeline is predictable: you meet someone early, have the big white wedding, take the dreamy honeymoon photos, land a great job, buy a place, and have kids, all before you're thirty.

This message might be casual in its delivery, but it is sharp and exacting in the required outcome. It is expected, and it is a given.

So I took it on board.

Not consciously, more like osmosis.

Everyone around me did too.

And that messaging, that process of osmosis, is not something you question when you're young. You just assume that's what life looks like if you're on track.

And because that timeline is repeated everywhere around you, eventually, you think you want it too. It seems like the natural choice.

There's a saying: 'you don't know what you don't know,' and in this case, it didn't even enter my head that there might have been other options available to me.

Looking back, I can admit this: I wanted that version of the life I was shown.

Not because it came from me... but because it was the only version we were ever presented with.

And somewhere deep down, without realising, I started keeping score.

By twenty-five, *this* should have happened.

By twenty-eight, *that*.

By thirty, *locked in, sorted, figured out*.

That imaginary clock?

It ticks for all of us.

Loudly.

When the Clock Finally Struck Truth

For me, the wake-up wasn't a single dramatic moment with violins playing and everything crashing down around me.

It was slower.

More like a creeping discomfort I kept trying to ignore… until I couldn't anymore.

But if I had to name the biggest catalyst, it's simple: COVID.

The COVID-19 pandemic hit the world when I was twenty-three.

And everything: careers, dating, travel, milestones, they all froze.

Three years of life put on ice.

Suddenly, I blinked, and I was twenty-six.

I had technically lived those years, but they didn't feel lived.

Not in the usual ways.

There were no progress markers, you know the ones: the graduation photo with cap and gown, the slightly unhinged European summer travel pics, the dazzling diamond engagement ring.

The milestones everyone uses to figure out where they stand compared to everyone else.

And that's when the anxiety kicked in.

The panic of being behind.

The sense that everyone else had moved forward, even if logically I knew they hadn't.

The pandemic didn't just put my social life on pause; it paused the fairytale timeline I'd been unconsciously measuring myself against.

And the strange part was that the timeline wasn't even realistic to begin with.

The pause made it obvious.

It shoved it in my face.

I realised the life I had expected, the one the world had told me to want, wasn't happening the way I thought it would.

And underneath that?

A deeper truth: I wasn't even sure I wanted it anymore.

But that understanding didn't feel empowering at the time. It felt like a loss. And it caused me a ton of anxiety. I lived under a black cloud; there was a constant sense of running out of time. A fear that I'd missed something, failed something, or fallen off the path.

COVID didn't create the cracks; they were always there. It just shone a torch on them.

Living by Expectations That Aren't Mine

Even now, the expectation that haunts me the most is the idea that by thirty, life should be sorted.

Not perfect, but at least clear.

By thirty, you are meant to have a stable partner, a thriving career, savings, a plan, a path.

A sense of certainty.

And honestly?

I know that a lot of women my age feel this. It's not just me.

The pressure is subtle but constant; it is the Spotify playlist in the background that never switches off.

Even when I tell myself I don't believe in the timeline anymore, it still has power over me.

There are days when I feel behind. Days when I think I'm running out of time. Days when I compare myself to people who seem to be ticking the boxes.

But I've learned to interrupt it.

I break out of those thoughts by talking to my friends: women who are also pushing against this invisible rulebook.

Women who remind me that the timeline was bullshit to begin with. Women who are rewriting their own version of life and letting go of the pressure to be perfect and sorted by some arbitrary age.

I join communities where these types of conversations are normal, places where women openly talk about expectations, pressure, burnout, career confusion, and fear.

Places where we are allowed to say, "I don't have it figured out yet," without feeling judged.

Those spaces give me breathing room.

They remind me that the fairytale isn't the standard; it is a story someone else wrote.

Love and Relationships: What I Thought *vs* What I Know Now

Growing up, love looked so simple.

Effortless.

Beautiful.

Clean.

Everything fit together, everything worked out, and everything felt magical.

Movies make it seem like relationships just happen, and if you meet the right person, it's smooth sailing.

No arguments. No awkward conversations. No doubts.

Just romance, certainty, and natural chemistry.

But real love?

Real relationships?

They are not the rom-com version.

I used to think love meant holding it all together, smoothing things over, keeping the boyfriend no matter what, swallowing your feelings, and just pushing through anything to keep the illusion of perfection alive.

Fuck the Fairytale: Find Your Own Magic

Now I know: Love is continuous communication.

Real check-ins.

Mutual respect.

Safety.

The kind where you don't have to pretend or shrink yourself.

And love includes compromise, the healthy kind, not the self-erasing kind.

I'm still learning how to do that.

I'm learning to speak up when something doesn't feel right, instead of forcing myself to play the cool girl role.

You know the one: nonchalant, devil-may-care.

The cool girl soundtrack goes something like this: "I'm far too sophisticated and worldly to appear needy and dependent." I actively choose to turn that soundtrack off.

Because I know that love isn't about holding your breath to keep the peace.

Love isn't about forcing a perfect picture.

Love isn't about performing.

Aligned love is quiet but strong.

Love is not public displays of affection put on just for show; it is a bond you feel without needing to display it.

And self-love?

That's the hardest one.

I've realised loving myself means doing the uncomfortable, honest work.

The stuff I don't want to do but know will make me better.

Saying no.

Setting boundaries.

Choosing alignment to my values over approval from others.

One example?

Leaving my first job (I'll get to that properly soon). It scared me, made me doubt myself, and the decision to leave felt like the opposite of a safe or logical choice.

But it was the best thing I could have done for myself.

It was me choosing growth over fear.

Money, Work and The Reality of Success

I grew up with the idea that careers were linear: you start somewhere good, you move up, you keep going.

Simple.

Straightforward.

Smooth.

And I genuinely believed that a high-quality life was achievable without too much struggle; all you had to do was follow the steps.

Then real life hit.

After graduating, I landed my first corporate job, and it wasn't long before the company went into crisis mode. The graduate experience I imagined, the one meant to set me up for my whole career?

It never happened.

Instead, I burned out. I felt lost. I couldn't see the next step.

Leaving that job after two years felt like failure.

I hadn't expected that at all.

I thought I'd climb the internal ladder in this company and build something steady.

But instead, I walked away with nothing lined up.

And the job search afterwards took longer than I expected.

Much longer.

Living in Sydney didn't help. The cost of living is insane. The financial pressure is real.

And the fear that financial pressure drives then sits under a lot of decisions:

'What if I choose wrong?'

'What if I fail?'

'What if I can't support myself?'

But I'm also in rooms full of women building careers, getting smart with their money, and levelling up their financial literacy.

And that keeps me lit up.

It reminds me that I'm allowed to want more, even if the fear continues to tag along.

Success, On My Own Terms

For me now, success isn't about the loud stuff. Not the job title, the bragging rights, not the image.

Success is feeling aligned.

It is trusting myself.

It is knowing that I am growing.

The real measures are: my health, being fulfilled, and checking in to see whether I feel energised by the life I'm living.

If those things are compromised, I know I'm in the wrong place.

And something I've stopped chasing?

Trying to be the smartest, loudest person in the room.

That's not success.

That's insecurity pretending to be confidence.

I would rather build real connections. Learn from people quietly. I would rather surround myself with people who bring out the best in me.

Do I have doubts about not succeeding?

Absolutely.

I fear not being able to afford the life I picture. I fear not being financially secure enough to walk away from anything that is misaligned with the life I know is for me. I fear not feeling fulfilled long-term. And I fear holding myself back and missing out on opportunities that could potentially change my life.

But I'm learning to act anyway.

Fear doesn't mean stop.

It just means take a moment to think about it.

Body, Health and Becoming Strong Instead of Small

Women's bodies come with expectations from the moment we're born. From childhood to adulthood, our bodies are treated like they owe something to the world, that they need to explain and excuse themselves.

Everywhere you look, there's pressure to be a certain size, look a certain way, and always be put together.

Your worth is most definitely tied up in your appearance.

My body story is a bit different.

I grew up as a competitive Irish Dancer. I trained six times a week. Strength, discipline, and technique were normal to me.

My body wasn't decorative, it was functional.

When I quit dancing at sixteen, everything changed.

No structure. No built-in movement. No sense of being good at something physical.

I struggled.

I had to relearn how to see my body as something valuable without the scores, without the rankings, without judges deciding if I was good enough.

It took a while.

But then CrossFit appeared, and it helped. A completely different sport, a completely different space. It taught me to aim for strength, not smallness.

Now, being strong means being connected to myself: physically, emotionally, spiritually. It means trusting my body to carry me through challenges. It boosts my confidence. It makes me proud.

And for my future self, strength means independence.

I want to build the foundations now that will let me age feeling capable and grounded.

When I let go of dancing, it wasn't as devastating as you might imagine; it was actually a relief.

My body needed the break.

But redefining who I was after leaving the sport taught me resilience. It showed me that I can rebuild, adapt, and find new ways to feel powerful.

Fairytale, Reality... and the Reconstruction

At some point, usually silent, usually inconvenient, the version of life you were sold doesn't fall apart; it just... splinters.

For me, it was a slow, creeping awareness that the life I thought I was supposed to have was not the life I actually wanted.

But the more important truth was this: I wasn't living the life that matched who I actually was.

It's wild how long you can carry a script that isn't yours.

Years. Decades, even.

You keep reciting lines someone else wrote.

Your mum, your nan, the women you admired, the friends who seemed to have it all.

There is a version of you that is sitting there, scared to want more.

And then one day you realise you're starring in a story you didn't audition for. That the 'more' you are chasing is not something you want at all.

For me, the splinters showed up in the smallest moment. I remember sitting in my car, my hands on the steering wheel, staring out at the road, and seeing a life that technically 'worked' but didn't actually feed me.

And I remember thinking: "Is this it? Is this my story?"

That was the moment the fairytale stopped having power over me.

It didn't crumble overnight.

But the seed was planted: You're not stuck. You're just conditioned.

And conditioning can be rewritten, brutally, honestly, and beautifully.

One decision at a time.

The Reality We Don't Post About

Nobody tells you how painful it is to outgrow the narrative you were raised on.

They don't tell you that choosing yourself sometimes feels like walking out of a burning building. You watch as everyone else stays seated, they insist "it's not that hot," and you wonder what the hell they are thinking, what can't they see?

They don't tell you that when you stop being the helper, the strong one, the one who just 'gets on with it,' people become uncomfortable.

They don't warn you that you'll be accused of being selfish.

Ungrateful.

Overly emotional.

Too ambitious.

Or the classic: You've changed.

Well… yeah. I bloody hope so.

And here's the kicker: The moment you stop playing out the fairytale script, you're not just breaking generational patterns, you are disrupting other people's comfort.

But their comfort is not your responsibility.

Your responsibility is this:

To live an honest life.

A life that's yours.

A life that doesn't suffocate you.

The Cost of Staying Quiet

Women are trained, subtly and not so subtly, to be grateful.

To shrink.

To keep the peace.

To be polite.

To not make a scene.

To be manageable.

My story shows exactly what happens when that training runs your life:

You swallow things that hurt.

You minimise your needs.

You accept the crumbs because you were told crumbs were a privilege.

You call chaos normal.

You make excuses for people who never earned the benefit of the doubt.

You run on empty, telling yourself you're fine.

You become fluent in 'it's not that bad.'

But it is that bad. It always was. You were just raised to tolerate it.

And the moment you stop tolerating, the moment you start telling the truth, even quietly, even to yourself, your world begins to shift.

It doesn't feel like power at first. It feels like guilt. Like fear. Like "who do I think I am?"

But here's the truth no one seems to teach you: Bravery doesn't always roar. Sometimes bravery is the quiet decision you make when you stop lying to yourself.

When You Finally Choose Yourself

Choosing yourself doesn't come with fireworks. It doesn't come with applause. You don't get a medal or a parade.

Instead, it comes with shaking hands, a dry mouth, and the kind of clarity that terrifies you because it's real, it's honest, and it's vulnerability in its rawest form.

You wake up and you know: I can't keep doing this. I can't keep shrinking. I can't keep living a life that feels like a half version of myself.

And then you do the hardest thing in the world: you choose yourself anyway.

Not because it's glamorous. Not because it's easy.

But because the alternative is staying stuck in a story that makes you disappear.

That's the thing about fairytales: the princesses get saved, but they never get to choose.

I chose.

And that's the part of my story that actually matters.

The Rebuild No One Sees

After the crack comes the rebuild.

And this is where the work happens.

Not the Instagram version, not the 'new me' montage, but the gritty, human, deeply unglamorous bits.

Rebuilding looks like: saying no when your whole body shakes; leaving relationships, jobs, or identities that don't fit; sitting with uncomfortable truths instead of numbing yourself; challenging the belief that you need to be 'easy' or 'grateful'; letting go of people who only loved the palatable version of you; relearning that you're allowed to take up space; allowing yourself to want more; and trusting your instincts even when others don't understand.

Growth isn't pretty. It's awkward. It's confrontational. It's emotional. It's messy.

Growth is real.

And the entire time, you will be walking blindfolded, hoping something better is out there, trusting in the universe, not because a happy ending is guaranteed, but because the alternative is staying loyal to a life that keeps you small.

That is courage.

It is quiet, it is daily, and it is deeply personal.

The Truth About Freedom

There is a part of the fairytale that is never spoken about.

Freedom isn't sparkly. Freedom is responsibility. Freedom is work. Freedom is choosing yourself over and over, even when it hurts.

It is not running into the sunset with a man who finally gets you.

It is waking up and saying: I refuse to betray myself today.

It is learning to trust your voice more than you trust the expectations placed on you.

It is knowing that you are allowed to want a soft life, a wild life, a quiet life, or a complex one, as long as it is the life you choose for yourself.

Freedom comes with consequences.

So does staying stuck.

Choose your consequences carefully.

The Woman You Become Once You Finally Get Unstuck

When you stop chasing the life you were told to want, you finally get to meet the woman you were always meant to become.

She's not polished.

She's not perfect.

She's not universally adored.

She's not easy.

She's honest. Grounded. Self-respecting. Emotionally literate.

She is protective of her peace, and she is selective with her energy.

She is compassionate but not naïve.

And she doesn't apologise for her boundaries.

This is the woman who grows when the old story finally collapses.

This is the woman who gets to build a life that makes sense, her kind of sense, not the world's.

This is the woman I am becoming.

Not the princess.

Not the damsel.

Not the people-pleaser.

Not the good girl.

I am becoming a woman who knows her worth, and I am becoming someone who refuses to shrink to make others comfortable.

So... Where to from Here?

Fairytales end at the wedding.

Right?

Wrong.

Real life begins at the awakening.

And my awakening, that quiet, grounded, deep moment of truth, is not an ending at all. It's a starting point.

Where you go from here depends on one thing: What story do you want to write, now that the old one doesn't fit?

This next chapter of your life isn't about rebellion for rebellion's sake.

It's about alignment. Integrity. Self-respect. Emotional safety.

Growth that is yours.

Not inherited, not predictable, not performed.

And the best part?

You don't need permission.

You don't need approval.

You don't need a hero.

You don't need to explain yourself.

Your life is yours now.

Mandy Merrifield

The pen is yours. The script is yours. The direction is yours.

The fairytale is dead.

Good.

Now you finally get to live.

A love letter to my younger self

Dear Cleo,

You deserve a big life.

Do not feel you need to fit into a box or a certain timeline, and do not feel like you are running out of time to get your life together.

Fill your life with people who support and love you, and do not change yourself to fit in with other people.

It will be hard not to be tempted to do this.

Keep doing things you are passionate about, even if they are not mainstream.

Stay authentic to yourself and trust your intuition.

You are strong and a force to be reckoned with, and anyone who tries to dampen that does not have a place in your life.

Keep showing up for yourself and for others.

Also, stop overplucking your eyebrows.

Please.

Find Your Own Magic: A Guided Reflection

Values that Light the Way. What Really Matters?

Take a deep breath. Place a hand on your heart.

Write your responses to each prompt:

- When I think of the moments I've felt most like 'me,' what was around me? Think of the people, the space, the sounds, the smells, the colours.

- What are the qualities I admire in people I love or look up to?

- If I stripped away the expectations and shoulds… what would still matter?

Look for the themes; that is where your values are going to reveal themselves.

The Joy Test

Ask yourself:

- What activities make me forget the time because I'm *honestly* happy?

- What kinds of conversations leave me energised, not depleted?

- Who in my life brings out the version of me I'm proud of?

Your values thrive where your joy lives.

The Gut Check

Values become loudest when they're violated.

Take some time to journal:

- What recent situations have left me frustrated or unsettled? Why?

- What value was being pushed against? (e.g., fairness, honesty, independence, fun)

This is not about blame; it is about clarity.

Choose Your Top Five Guiding Values

From everything above, choose five that feel like home.

Here is a list to help you. This is not exhaustive; it is simply here for inspiration:

- Courage
- Connection
- Freedom
- Kindness
- Adventure
- Creativity
- Stability
- Playfulness
- Respect
- Authenticity
- Joy
- Love
- Learning
- Compassion
- Beauty
- Community
- Confidence
- Balance

Three Lenses

Now let's look through three lenses.

What do these values look like in action?

What words do you say or hear?

What behaviours do you see or action?

Which body gestures and facial expressions do you cultivate, or see, in others?

What is the tone of voice you hear or speak? What is the internal monologue?

Let's use *kindness* as our example: What do you see when…

1. You are being *kind* to others?

2. Others are being *kind* to you?

3. You are being *kind* to yourself?

Chapter 5:
Choices

Cake, Alcohol and the Line in the Sand

Choice.

There is a word we have all heard before.

And what I am about to tell you is no secret.

We can all choose what we want: an option that pleases the most people, or one that is for our own pure pleasure.

We can choose the easy way, or the one that creates the least conflict or tension.

You can choose to have a second piece of cake, or not.

You can choose to go to the gym or go for a walk today, or you can choose not to.

You can choose to have long or short hair, wear a wig, colour your hair, or go grey. You can choose the clothes you want to wear and whether to use make-up.

Sometimes our choices are not easy.

And sometimes it isn't as simple as not having more cake.

Sometimes we have to choose between a shitty choice and an even shittier one.

After I got sober, I was broke, I was in debt, and I had no job.

How on earth did I get back on my feet?

Well, I put my pride aside, and I made some choices.

I chose to take a cleaning job; cleaning men's urinals in a caravan park was part of that experience, and I can assure you, it was as disgusting as it sounds.

I chose to work on weekends and evenings after my day job in a retail gig paying minimum wage, even though I was a highly skilled and qualified professional.

I chose to freeze my arse off, working early mornings in a coffee van on sports fields, whipped by icy blasts every single Sunday morning.

Did I like having to do this?

No.

But what was the other choice?

Bankruptcy.

And most likely, never getting back on my feet.

I didn't like that choice. From my perspective, bankruptcy was the worse choice.

For those of you who haven't worked it out, I am a recovered and long-term sober alcoholic. At my worst, I was drinking up to eight bottles of red wine a day.

As a result, I lost everything.

My precious daughters were the biggest casualty, for me and for them.

What they went through, I will never fully understand, and they will likely carry the emotional scars for life.

I wish it were different.

I do not have a time machine.

But if I did, I would never have chosen to pick up that glass of wine.

I would have chosen not to buy into the 'mummy deserves a wine culture' that was pervasive in the early 2000s.

I would have chosen to face my demons much earlier than I did, and I would have decided to do something about the niggling feeling that I knew I had a problem.

I would have chosen to leave my marriage earlier.

Before the unhappiness, the lack of fulfilment, and the feeling of being trapped became too much.

I would have chosen to leave before the depression got so bad that I used alcohol to numb it.

Hindsight is a wonderful thing.

I will never forgive myself for the experience my girls went through as a result of my alcoholism. I do not care a flying fuck for the people who tell me 'I have to.'

Who on earth could forgive themselves for that?

I do forgive myself for other things though. And as a result, I make different choices today.

It is what I have done every day since the 13th of October 2016.

I choose to try to be a better person.

I choose to show up for the people who need me, want me, and love me.

I choose to love my daughters unconditionally, and to hold the fierce, unwavering hope that one day our relationships might be different.

I choose to help others through coaching, hypnotherapy, writing, building supportive communities and networks for women, and by sharing my story.

I choose to replace wine with soda. As a dear friend said to me in the very early days of my sobriety, "Choose to put a different liquid in the glass." Done.

I choose to go for a walk with my dog rather than have a drink.

I choose to get help through therapy, rather than drowning or numbing my sorrows.

I choose to try to see the many sides of a story or a situation, even though sometimes that situation or that story hurts.

I choose to be open-minded. I work hard every day to be patient, kind, caring, and generous with my love.

I choose to relax and find joy in ways other than unwinding at the end of the day with a glass of wine.

I choose to own my shit.

I choose to schwog (shuffle-jog-walk) because I can't run. My daughter coined that term, and I love it. A few years ago, I schwogged the City to Surf in Sydney. The pride I felt in myself as my body literally fell down the hill into Bondi is something I will never be able to explain fully.

I choose to live my life as best I can, which means not choosing to numb feelings of sadness and loss with alcohol. I also choose a healthier way to celebrate when something goes right, which I am happy to say is often these days.

I do not define myself by that particular chapter in my life. It is a part of my story, though.

Do I wish it hadn't happened?

Of course.

If it hadn't happened, I wouldn't be the person I am today.

Or maybe I would have got here another way, who knows? The universe works in mysterious ways.

I also make a very conscious choice to be loud about sobriety, for those who aren't as bold as I am.

Have I faced backlash? Yes.

Have I lost people along the way? Yes.

This is what I have learned: When you make big choices, it will show you who your real friends are, and who are not.

And often, that doesn't have anything to do with you. It is simply that when you put a boundary in place, when you choose to respect yourself, when you choose to say no to something that no longer serves you, what it does is hold up a mirror to your critics.

And that mirror reflects their behaviour, their lack of boundaries, their bad habits, their lack of self-respect.

As a general rule, I've found that many people don't like that mirror, so I've let them go easily. It opens up space in my life for the people who see me as I am today and who love me, flaws and all.

And for those who continue to mistreat me, I will ask you to look in that mirror. Really take a good, hard look.

If you see someone who is looking back at you who is perfect, who has never, ever made a mistake in their life, who has never fucked up, who has never disappointed anyone, told a lie (big or small), or hurt anyone (on purpose or unintentionally), well, I deserve your continued hate and contempt.

With all my love, and every single one of my blessings, go for it. Continue to treat me like dirt under your feet.

I don't think that perfect person exists. I am certainly far from perfect, and I have never pretended to be.

There are other choices we get to make as adults. One of the most powerful, I think, is to draw a line in the sand and move on.

You can spend your life blaming others for what has happened to you. You can let it define your life and consume you with anger, hurt, and victimhood.

Or you can choose to say, "It happened, and I choose to live life on my terms and to the fullest I can."

I have scoliosis, and I have one lung. The scoliosis appears to be genetic, passed down through that long line of strong women I referred to at the beginning of this book. I wore a god-awful back brace through most of my teenage years, and it was horrific, mortifying, almost catastrophic to my younger sense of self.

The lung issue, well, that's another story.

I could spend my life feeling sorry for myself, or I can actively choose to make the best of what I have.

This is what I choose to do. I work hard to strengthen my body so it can carry me as best it can into my later years.

I can walk for hours on end, but give me a steep hill and I'm screwed. My lung doesn't cope with elevations; it tightens in my chest to a point of immense, 'I think I'm having a heart attack' fear-inducing pain. It is why, when I hike the Camino de Santiago next October for my ten-year soberversary, I have chosen the route with the fewest hills and the gentlest gradient.

Am I angry, upset, or woe-is-me, because I had to make this choice about my trip?

Are you fucking kidding me? I am going to be hiking through Portugal and Spain with one of my oldest and dearest friends. It will be a pinch-me, surreal, and all-around incredible experience.

Here's the thing about choices, folks. You make them, you own them, and you, for the most part, control them.

Yes, there will be situations where you don't have a choice, and I acknowledge that.

Life is ten per cent what happens to you, and ninety per cent how you respond.

So it may not be a choice between roses or tulips; it may not be a simple choice, like deciding to drink more water today. But you will always have a choice.

Very early on in my sobriety, on the first Christmas Day, someone said, "I can't believe you can't even have a drink."

My response went something like this:

"I can choose to do whatever I want. I have a car, I have keys, I have two legs and a heartbeat, and I know how to drive. I can get in my car right now and buy as many bottles of wine as I like, but I am choosing not to. I am choosing my girls, my life, my career, and my health. I am choosing me."

Remember that.

Find Your Own Magic: A Guided Reflection

Using the Choice Point®

Here's a reflection exercise based on the Choice Point® model from Acceptance and Commitment Therapy (ACT®). It is for personal use only. If you need support, please reach out to an accredited practitioner.

Please note that the model is trademarked.

For this guided reflection, we are going to use a super-simplified 'Mandy' version.

What is your goal?

You can use the SMART goal framework if you like:

- Be SPECIFIC about what your goal is
- Make your goal MEASURABLE
- Ask yourself: how ACHIEVABLE is this goal?
- Is this goal RELATIVE to your bigger picture life?
- What is the TIMEFRAME you want to achieve your goal in?

Instructions

Every day, every minute, every second, we make choices.

Using this very simplified version of the Choice Point® model… you get to make those choices that either move you towards your goal, or move you away from it.

Example

Goal: I want to get up at 6am every morning to walk my dog (at the moment, I get up at 7am)

Scenario 1: Alarm goes off… It's raining outside

Choice *towards* my goal: I get up, grab an umbrella and off I go. How good am I going to feel knowing that I kept this promise to myself?

Choice *away* from my goal: I can hear the rain on the roof, I roll over and go back to sleep, saying, "I'll start tomorrow".

Neither is wrong, neither is right… you do you.

But please…

Think about why your goal is important to you, and what it adds to the bigger picture of your life.

Big changes are made one step at a time, as they say, 'Rome wasn't built in a day.'

And please, darling girl, remember: tomorrow is never promised. Make the most of the day in front of you.

Notes

I have used an extremely modified and simplified version of the Choice Point® model. If you would like more information on this model, please visit: www.actmindfully.com.au.

If this exercise brings up strong distress, upsetting memories, or feelings beyond your comfort zone, it may help to work with a trained ACT® therapist.

Rachel: Learning to Enjoy the Ride

The Fairytale I Had to Outgrow

I grew up believing in the storybook version of life, the kind with castles, tiaras, and happy-ever-afters written in perfect cursive.

I read all the fairytales.

I memorised the rhythm of rescue.

Prince Charming would find me, adore me, and take care of me.

I wanted to be the princess, but a modern one, the kind who could have both sides of life: the ball gown *and* the career, the love *and* the independence.

My parents made that story look both achievable and confusing.

My dad was the breadwinner, and my mum ran a restaurant. On the surface, they had the perfect picture.

Partnership, purpose, family.

Behind the scenes, it was dysfunction dressed as domesticity. They taught me, without ever saying it aloud, that love meant walking on eggshells, and that normal was chaos with a slick of cherry red lipstick slapped on.

The irony of my story is that I word-for-word, detail-for-detail, recreated the exact same farcical picture.

My first marriage could have been a mirror of theirs: controlling, volatile, and full of the same silences and explosions I swore I'd never repeat. I remember looking at my four boys and thinking, I can't let them grow up believing this is how you treat a woman.

But the damage had already started to thread its way through; those learned patterns, those quiet echoes of what I had accepted as normal for far too long.

I believed the problem was me.

If I just tried harder, spoke softer, smiled more, he'd change. 'He' being my first husband.

That's what happens when the fairytale gets under your skin: you mistake perseverance for love and silence for peace.

You start to think that staying is strength, even when it's slowly undoing you.

The truth started to unravel in tiny moments.

Not a big bang, just a slow dawning.

The quote that stuck with me was: 'Sunshine all the time creates a desert.'

And that is what I had been chasing: constant harmony, constant happiness.

But life, real life, has storms and shadows. I had been trying to build a garden in denial of this.

The turning point wasn't glamorous.

It came wrapped in exhaustion and postnatal depression; a fog I couldn't lift myself out of.

I felt invisible in my own home.

My family didn't see it, my husband didn't care to, and I didn't have the words yet to call it what it was: coercive control.

Then, almost accidentally, I found my voice. It came through a Party Plan business. I signed up thinking it would simply be a short-term distraction, but it turned out to be the lifeline I didn't know I needed.

For the first time in years, I was surrounded by women who saw me, encouraged me, and believed I could stand on my own. Every product demonstration, every meeting, every small win started to rebuild the self-esteem I had been talked out of.

That business became my stepping stone, not just to financial independence, but emotional freedom. It gave me something no fairytale ever mentioned: the power to rescue myself.

Fuck the Fairytale: Find Your Own Magic

Leaving my marriage came at a cost: financial, emotional, and mental.

My family didn't understand.

They thought I had absolutely lost the plot and that I was destroying a perfectly good life.

My mother, bless her, in her own warped way, sided with my husband. She would go to his house, clean for him, take him flowers, and check in.

Meanwhile, I was alone and left to piece myself together. To make it worse, he continued to tell our sons lies about me.

It broke me in ways that still ache, but I learned something crucial from that pain: sometimes freedom feels like loss before it feels like peace.

And because the universe has a dark sense of humour, I went and did it again.

My second marriage, different man, same pattern.

Another version of coercive control, wrapped in a different accent.

That was my wake-up call: it wasn't just about who I chose, it was about why. I kept picking men who mirrored the chaos I had been taught to normalise.

As that moment of truth landed, everything changed. That is when I stopped chasing the fantasy and started writing something real.

I can say now, after years of therapy, rebuilding, and hard truths, that I am finally in a relationship that feels like freedom.

Not perfect, not polished, but mine.

A partnership where I can breathe, and where I'm not shrinking to fit someone else's story.

But the fairytale script, the patterns, the subconscious messages and learnings, these things don't easily leave you. They linger in the small things: the way I still feel like I'm not quite good enough, the voice that tells me to be presentable, and to never, ever, leave the house unless I'm fully made up.

My mother, beautiful and image-obsessed, left that imprint deep. She was the kind of woman people turned to look at, and I was the girl standing beside her, wondering if I would ever measure up. I remember my first boyfriend, and him telling me how stunning my mum was. That kind of comparison doesn't fade; it embeds itself in your forever reflection.

That reflection has loosened its grip over time, but if I am honest, it still sits in the back of my mind.

The perfectionism, the performance.

It's a ghost that constantly floats just behind my consciousness: you're not enough unless you're immaculate.

Will I ever fully break free of this? I don't know.

But I have learned to see it for what it is: conditioning, not truth.

Love, for me, used to mean endurance. I grew up believing that relationships were supposed to be messy, that men could treat women poorly and still be good men.

Apologies weren't part of the vocabulary.

And with these beliefs, I carried this pattern into every partnership I had, continually mistaking tolerance for loyalty.

Both of my marriages looked perfect from the outside, curated, shiny, right. And yet behind the smiles and matching Christmas cards, I was disappearing.

When I finally walked away from that second marriage, the world clapped politely from the sidelines, people saying they'd always known he wasn't right for me.

Hindsight does not count for help. I think sometimes they say it to make themselves feel better about not speaking up sooner.

The truth is, I stayed too long because I didn't want to fail at the story I'd been handed. I wanted to make it work, to fix it, to be the woman who could hold everything together.

But once I knew it was over, I was done.

When I go, I go.

There's no halfway.

The aftermath was brutal: emotionally draining, financially terrifying, lonely as hell.

There were nights I almost went back just to stop the ache.

But I didn't.

I stayed the course.

Walking Away and Freedom

Healing was not a straight line.

It was more like trying to build a house on land that had already been burned to the ground; the earth beneath me was fragile and unpredictable.

To rebuild, to start again, I had to clear out the debris, the rubbish, the remnants of everything I had believed about love, worth, and womanhood.

For a long time, I thought healing meant forgiving everyone else: my exes, my parents, even my younger self who had stayed too long.

But the real work wasn't in forgiving them.

It was in forgiving myself for not knowing better, for confusing love with survival, for mistaking control for care. I had been trained to believe that if you loved someone hard enough, you could fix them. The truth is, sometimes the most loving thing you can do is leave.

It took years to learn that walking away doesn't make you heartless; it makes you conscious. It means you've stopped trying to rewrite someone else's story and that you have finally made the choice to start writing your own.

I look back now and realise that I wasn't failing at love. I was just outgrowing the version of love I'd been sold, the version that told me I had to earn affection, perform femininity, and stay small so I wouldn't make anyone uncomfortable. The version that made me think being chosen was the prize, when in reality, the prize had always been to choose myself.

There's a special kind of freedom that comes when you stop performing. When you can finally walk into a room without the armour of makeup and perfection, without trying to prove your value through what you give or how well you hold everything together. I still love feeling beautiful; that hasn't changed, but the reason behind it has.

I don't get ready for anyone else anymore.

I do it for me.

I deserve to feel good in my own skin, not because someone else needs me to look the part.

Learning to Say No

I used to think patterns were just coincidences, bad luck in love.

Now I see them for what they are: invitations to wake the hell up.

Every man I chose was a reflective mirror for what was not healed within me.

The control, the criticism, the emotional withholding, all of it reflected the wounds I hadn't dared to face.

Once I stopped asking, "Why do they keep doing this to me?" and started asking, "Why do I keep choosing it?" everything shifted.

That question became my compass.

It's brutal, asking yourself why you're drawn to pain disguised as passion.

Why does stability feel boring when you grew up in chaos?

Why do nice guys make you uneasy?

Calm feels foreign when all you've ever known is walking on eggshells.

This is where the real work lives.

In the discomfort. In the mirror.

I started seeing the pattern everywhere, not just in men, but in friendships, family dynamics, and even business partnerships. I was a magnet for people who wanted to take up space without offering any in return. And every time I said yes to their needs before my own, I was unconsciously confirming that my worth was negotiable.

So I started saying no.

Not loudly, not with fireworks, just quietly, consistently.

No to one-sided relationships.

No to apologising for existing.

No to playing small so someone else could feel big.

Each small 'no' started building a new kind of power, the type of power that does not require permission.

Love and a Cup of Tea

For the first time in my life, I'm in a relationship that doesn't feel like survival.

It feels like a partnership, the kind where two people meet as equals, not saviour and saved.

It is not about fixing or performing.

It is about being.

It's funny though; when you've spent most of your life in chaos, peace can feel suspicious.

For the longest time, I kept waiting for the other shoe to drop, for the argument that would confirm my old story: that love always hurts, and that happiness is temporary.

But it didn't come.

I had to learn to sit with that.

It was hard.

I had to rewire myself to believe that love could be calm. That it could be kind. That it could exist without drama.

To quote the old Pantene advertisement, 'it didn't happen overnight'.

It took unlearning years of conditioning, the conditioning that comes from parents, movies, glossy magazines, and media, and relearning that sometimes the most romantic thing you can do for yourself is to stop chasing intensity and start choosing peace.

Real love doesn't need fireworks every day.

It is steady, and it is safe.

It is the cup of tea waiting for you after a long day, the silence that feels like home, the conversation where you can say the messy things and not be punished for it.

That's the love I have now.

Not perfect, but real.

And here's the wild part: when I stopped needing love to save me, it found me differently. It met me at eye level.

Motherhood: The Mirror and the Motivation

Being a mum was the thing that finally broke the illusion of perfection for me.

I couldn't unsee the reflection of myself in my boys' eyes: the confusion, the tension, the lessons they were absorbing without words. I knew that if I stayed in that relationship, the one with their dad, my first husband, I wasn't just teaching them how to treat women. I was teaching them how to be a man.

And that is what finally did it for me.

Not the pain, not the loneliness, but the realisation that my silence would become their blueprint.

I still carry guilt about that time. The yelling, the crying, the pretending. I thought I was protecting them by holding it together. I see now that what I was really doing was showing them how to abandon themselves, and I refuse to let that be their inheritance.

They see a different version of me now, a woman who stands tall in her truth, who apologises when she needs to, but never for existing.

They see a woman who works hard not to repeat the patterns that once trapped her.

I want them to grow up knowing that love is respect, not control. That strength and softness can coexist.

And maybe, one day, they'll choose women who don't have to heal from men like their father.

I Am Woman

Sometimes I still catch myself apologising out of habit, for taking up space, for having needs, for not being endlessly accommodating.

And then I remember: that's not who I am anymore.

I am not the woman waiting to be chosen.

I am not the woman who makes herself small so others feel big.

I am not the girl who mistakes chaos for passion.

I am the woman who rebuilt her life from the ground up.

Who chose peace over performance.

Who finally stopped mistaking scraps for sustenance.

And maybe that's the real moral of the story here: not that love is a fairytale, but that you get to write your own damn story.

Because I am not the damsel.

I am the damn storyline.

And that's how I started to learn what love actually looks like.

Love is not dependent on a man to validate your existence. Love is not quiet obedience or self-erasure.

Love is growing without guilt.

Love is strength without apology.

And that is my storyline for living happily ever after.

A love letter to my younger self

Dear Rachel,

Your life is going to bring joy and happiness, with some sorrow and heartbreak.

Remember always that you are capable of more than you realise.

Forget about others' opinions and society's view.

Dig deep and be the authentic you.

You don't need a man to feel worthy; you can do it on your own.

You are one million times stronger than you think, and can achieve anything if you can remove the thoughts in your head telling you that you aren't good enough.

Start reciting positive affirmations to yourself, because this is how you will create your future.

Your thoughts are powerful and prophetic.

You can create the future of your dreams with your thoughts.

Don't ever hold back!

This is your life. Live it wholeheartedly, enjoy the ride.

It's incredible and so fulfilling.

Chapter 6:
The Fairytale of Thin

In the 1990s, tucked between grunge, boy bands, and CD compilations, a quieter, fiercer fairytale slipped into women's lives: thin equals value, visibility equals belonging.

We were told that if we just became the right kind of body, slim, tall, angular, with our bones poking out, we had arrived.

We would be chosen.

We would matter.

And the fairytale very clearly stated: have that body, and the rest will follow.

For those of you who join me as a hallowed member of Generation X, you might remember Kate Winslet of *Titanic* fame. On that oh-so-unforgiving red carpet, Kate was subjected to brutal commentary about her body.

Reporters joked she looked 'a little melted and poured into' her dress, and one even went so far as to say she should have worn two sizes larger.

Kate Winslet was talented, celebrated, and still not thin enough for the lens that valued her body more than her artistry. She once recalled that at acting school she was told, "If you're going to look like this, you'll have to settle for the fat-girl parts."

In film and fiction, and in the world of the 1990s in general, the message was constant: nothing tastes as good as skinny feels.

The mantra of an entire generation.

Sacrifice became virtue.

Take our dear Bridget Jones; she was smart, witty and deeply human, yet she still carried the burden of weight as the sub-plot of her acceptability. Bridget was the star of the show, yet the narrative kept pulling her back to size, shape, and weight.

On the supermodel runways and in the glossy pages of magazines, thin wasn't just an aesthetic; thin was necessary.

Heroin chic.

Size zeros were trophies. We saw models who had thighs that did not touch, visible ribs, and narrow hips.

Naomi Campbell and the other supermodels of the day strode and strutted, giving the world an image of the female body so thin it excluded nearly all of us.

Magazines, television, Hollywood, the fashion runways of Paris, Milan and New York all told us the ideal body was our entrance ticket.

Thinness equalled control, youth, worth.

And then there were the pregnancy bounce-back rituals.

When a star had a baby, the headline that quickly followed was, 'Will she lose weight?'

Who remembers Posh Spice being weighed on live TV just six months after giving birth in 1999?

The camera leaned in. The scales became spectacle. The story was: you had a baby, now shrink.

Be desirable again.

The Cost of the '90s Fairytale

Many of us still carry this with us today.

When your appearance becomes your identity, the cost is high.

Imagine living the message that your body, your shape, your size, your visible frame, is the condition for your value.

Ageing is failure.

Weight gain is shameful.

And real women in their 20s and 30s swallowed the script: diet, fast, restrict.

Wake Up, it is 2025

Women have thankfully begun waking up to the cost of that '90s hellish fairytale.

What if your worth is not in your measurements?

What if your body is not your currency but the vessel in which to experience a magnificent life?

What if ageing is proof of living, not a loss of value?

What if strength, voice, and intelligence matter far more than your waist size?

Kate Winslet has recently reflected on her experience; she confronted the press while looking back at those red carpet moments, saying, "I hope this haunts you."

Victoria Beckham speaks openly about her struggles with the eating disorder and weight shame she suffered through.

The script is now shifting.

Representation has now broadened.

And conversations are starting to change.

Women are declaring the fairytale for today: I am not my body, I am my story.

Appearance does not make us who we are as women.

The '90s fairytale promised that if you had the body, it would unlock the life.

It lied.

Yes, our bodies matter. They house our lives. They carry our stories. But they do not define them.

We are more than pretty shapes.

We are more than frames.

We are story-makers.

We are worth more than the world told us we were.

And when you tell that to yourself, loud and clear, every day, something transforms.

Rewriting the Story

For the reader carrying the '90s body fairytale in their bones, let us rewrite it together.

Start by naming the myth.

When you hear in your mind: 'I'll be happy when I'm thinner,' recognise whose voice that is.

Claim your worth beyond your body. Your value lives in your words, your curiosity, your kindness, your presence. Not your size.

Cultivate your body for you, not for spectacle.

Eat. Move. Rest.

Because you live in this body.

Change the mirror-conversation. When you look in the mirror, ask yourself: how did I live today?

Don't ask: how did I look?

Give your future self permission. The body you are in now is enough, the one ageing, doing, loving, and carrying life.

Honour it.

Find Your Own Magic: A Guided Reflection

What Does Appearance Mean to You?

This space is just for you, my darling, not for the camera, not for the crowd, not for anyone else.

So, let's take a breath together. Settle down into your body, the one that has carried you through every single day of being alive.

And let's ask some questions.

What did the world teach me about beauty?

What messages about my body did I absorb growing up?

Whose voice became the critic in my own head?

Which movies, magazines, or people made me believe "better" was always skinnier, smaller, softer, prettier?

Take note of any moments that still feel sharp. And remember, you have survived them, and today is a new day.

What has my body helped me do?

Consider the life you have lived inside this skin.

What joy has my body given me?

What moments of strength, laughter, intimacy, or movement prove its worth?

Who has this body hugged, held, raised, protected, or loved?

What is one belief about appearance I am ready to let go of?

Examples:

- I need to be smaller to be admired.
- My face must not age.
- My beauty is my value.

Write your own.

Then rewrite it with truth: I am worth more than my reflection.

How do I want to feel in my body?

Not how you want it to look, how you want to live in it.

Choose words that lift you:

- Strong
- Free
- Desired
- Safe
- Alive
- Powerful
- Playful
- Enough

Let these be the goals, not a number.

What daily gestures of respect can I offer this body?

- Feed it when it's hungry
- Rest when it's tired
- Move in ways that feel joyful
- Dress it for comfort and confidence
- Speak to it like someone you love

Self-kindness becomes a habit with gentle practice.

A Note to Yourself

I do not owe the world pretty.

I owe myself presence, pleasure, and peace.

My appearance is one small part of me, not the whole story.

I am allowed to take up space.

I am allowed to grow and age.

I am allowed to love who I see.

I am enough.

A Note from Mandy

I have recently started going to the gym, three to five times a week. I want to lose a little weight.

WTF Mandy???? Haven't you just finished telling us all that life isn't about a number?

Yes, indeed, I have.

Here's the thing, girls.

I have one lung. I was born with one and a half lungs, and the half has shrivelled over the last 51 years.

And as a teenager, I wore a Boston back brace for about three years due to a severe curvature of my spine. It is called scoliosis. My back doesn't just curve; it resembles a chicken twistie as the vertebrae edge up from my pelvic bones to my neck.

After I lost my dad last year, I got really sick, probably from stress. An X-ray of my lung revealed that I didn't have pneumonia (thank goodness), but it did show that my back is starting to fuse. Side note: this is why I have begun to shrink, and why when I did a body scan mid last year, I had a stand-up argument with the technician, who adamantly told me I was 158cm, not 160.2cm (which was my height when the brace came off… that is a story for another day).

Anyhow, a bit of peri- or menopausal weight gain (not quite sure where I am in that cycle), along with this back fusion, was making it very hard for me to get out of bed in the morning. Nothing drastic, it just hurt like hell.

The solution?

Looking after and strengthening this unique, quirky, and spectacular body of mine.

Because…

I want to travel.

I want to be active.

I want to walk my dog.

I want to be the cool grandma if and when grandbabies come along.

It is not about a number.

And so, I have a 22-year-old personal trainer who is fabulous. It is fun. I am enjoying getting strong again.

And not only is it good for my body, but it is excellent for my mind. As someone who has experienced deep, dark depression and who probably will always have it lurking in the background, exercise and movement are crucial for me.

I intend to live life to the fullest.

So, don't mind me, just hanging out over here, being proactive in making that happen.

Mandy Merrifield

Eira: Walking Sunshine

The Standard Life

Growing up in a small town, the story was already written before I even arrived.

You didn't need to ask what came next; it was the same script handed to every girl who made it through Year 12.

Go to university.

Get a decent job.

Meet someone nice.

Get married in your twenties.

Have kids before thirty.

Buy a house.

Be grateful.

That was the rhythm of life, as natural and expected as breathing.

I didn't question it, not really. No one told me directly that you had to do it this way; it was just how things were done.

My sister followed it. My mum followed it. My Nan followed it.

However, my Nan did end up being the family exception. After my Pop died, she remarried. This simultaneously caused scandal and admiration. People gossiped; you couldn't have another bite at the cherry, no matter the circumstances.

Looking back, I think that's where the cracks in the fairytale first showed up for me, not that I noticed them at the time. While my Nan didn't live according to other people's rules or expectations, she still stuck loosely within the confines of the fairytale.

I didn't know it at the time, but the role modelling I received from my Nan, who said women could choose differently, would one day come back to change everything for me.

Fuck the Fairytale: Find Your Own Magic

And when my time came, I totally fractured the fucking thing.

The lines of the fairytale my Nan had loosened, I smashed apart.

Where did the story come from, those pressures and expectations?

Oh… everywhere!

Family, school, friends, the magazines scattered around hair salons, and the perfectly filtered lives on early Instagram.

It wasn't some dramatic indoctrination; it was just what everyone did.

You didn't have to dream it up; it was already dreamt for you.

The right path was safe, steady, and respectable, especially in a town where everyone knew everyone's business.

And so I followed it.

I finished school.

I went to university.

I found someone who ticked enough boxes: kind, reliable, ready for the next chapter.

We married when I was twenty-six.

It all looked right on paper.

I told myself this was comfort.

Adulthood done properly.

Little did I know that comfort, when built for someone else's life, could become a cage.

And then I remembered my Nan.

There wasn't some dramatic movie-moment epiphany.

It wasn't an affair or a big fight.

It was just one ordinary weekend in January, sunlight pouring through the window, quiet in my house. My husband was off camping with his mates, and I spent the weekend doing things I loved: slow mornings, walking, catching up with friends, and simply not having to check in with anyone.

And somewhere between my morning coffee on that day and the lazy afternoon that followed, it hit me.

Lightness. Freedom.

This was what happiness actually felt like.

Then came the harder truth: most of my life hadn't been built around moments like this. It had been built around him, my husband.

His plans.

His preferences.

His idea of the dream.

That realisation was brutal in its simplicity. I wasn't happy. I was running on the hamster wheel of a life that was never designed for my pleasure.

I was twenty-eight when I left.

Two years of marriage and a lifetime of pretending I was fine.

People think freedom starts the day you walk away, but it doesn't.

Freedom starts the day you tell yourself the truth, even if you're not ready to do anything about it yet.

Walking away from my marriage towards freedom wasn't glamorous.

It wasn't empowering, not at first.

It was messy, lonely, and full of guilt.

I was worried about what people would say: the whispers, the gossip, the pity, the 'but you had such a good life!' comments.

I felt like I was breaking something sacred. But deep down, I knew the only thing I was breaking was the illusion that this version of happiness was for everyone.

Emotionally, it was draining.

Socially, it was isolating.

Personally, though, it was the beginning of something raw and real.

It was the start of learning that freedom doesn't always come with fireworks. Sometimes, it comes with an empty house and the quiet sound of your own breathing when you finally stop performing.

The Fairytale That Almost Fitted

If I'm honest, the fairytale did fit, for a while.

I liked the security, the structure, the sense of belonging. It was easier to follow the plan than to question it. But as I had more and more life experiences, travelling, working, meeting different people, I started to see how often I bent myself to fit other people's wants.

I compromised constantly.

Going along with activities I didn't enjoy.

Saying yes to things that drained me.

Staying in a marriage longer than I should have because I didn't want to disappoint anyone.

I even held off on travelling because it wasn't something my now ex-husband wanted to do.

And when people asked if I wanted kids, I said yes because it was expected, even though I wasn't sure.

Now, when I think about those compromises, I realise they weren't small. They were the quiet kind that chip away at who you are. It wasn't one moment that broke the illusion. It was a thousand small ones, each time I swallowed a truth to keep the peace.

Inherited Expectations

Even now, the echoes of that story linger.

I catch myself thinking: "I need to have kids soon, or it'll be too late."

The old narrative doesn't disappear just because you reject it; it hides in your thoughts, waiting, and it makes you doubt your choices.

When it creeps in, I go for a walk.

I let myself breathe and remember that just because my version of life looks different to other people's, it doesn't mean it's wrong.

My life is a work in progress, and I remind myself daily that ticking boxes doesn't measure happiness; it's about how aligned my life feels with my truth.

Love and the Lies We're Sold

I grew up believing love was supposed to be perfect.

Effortless.

The kind of love that made everything fall into place.

It isn't anyone's fault; it has been like this since the beginning of time. It is just the story woven into the fabric of our lives.

It is the Disney ending, the happy couple who always look blissfully content.

But real love isn't a performance at a magical theme park.

Real love isn't measured by sparkles, or fireworks, or happy cartoon characters dancing in the streets.

Real love is not measured by how good it looks from the outside. It is measured in how safe, seen, and respected you feel on the inside.

I didn't know that back then, when I was in that particular relationship.

So what did I do?

I did everything I could to make my love story look right, even when I knew it wasn't.

That pattern continued even after my marriage ended.

I have stayed in two relationships because they looked good from the outside. The first was my marriage: the classic fairytale script. We'd been together since we were young. Married at twenty-six. He was thirty. Everyone said we were perfect.

But perfect doesn't mean compatible.

He wanted the house, the wife, the kids.

I wanted the world.

I remember sitting him down and saying, "We're not meant for each other." He understood, which somehow made it even sadder.

Then there was the second relationship, two years after my divorce.

The first few months were bliss, the kind of intoxicating start that makes you believe maybe this time it's going to be different. But slowly, things changed. He became controlling and emotionally abusive. He dictated how I looked, when I could see my friends, and accused me of cheating every time he was away.

It's wild how love can disguise control as care.

I didn't see it clearly until my friends stepped in.

They were the mirror I couldn't hold up to myself.

Their honesty saved me.

I'll be forever grateful for that.

For a while after that, my definition of love was bitter.

I saw it as something dangerous, something that took more than it gave. But then I met my current partner, and slowly, my definition started to shift.

We communicate openly.

He supports me, always.

He makes me feel special, not because he has to, but because it is who he is.

It's simple, and it's real.

Through him, and through my family and friends, I have learned that love doesn't need to be grand or perfect. It just needs to be honest.

Most importantly, I've learned to love myself differently.

I've learned to forgive myself for staying too long in relationships that didn't fit me, for not knowing better sooner, and for having to learn the hard way.

Now I know: love that is aligned doesn't ask you to shrink. It expands you. It makes space for who you're becoming, not just who you were.

The Currency of Success

I grew up with the idea that success came with a payslip.

That wealth meant stability, and stability meant worth.

It wasn't something my family ever said out loud; it was just how life looked.

Everyone worked in government or something secure, and they were respected for it.

Money meant you were doing life properly.

So, naturally, I followed suit.

I went to university, I got a good job, I climbed a bit, and ultimately, I stayed too long in places that burned me out.

In my hometown, two career categories made people nod approvingly: jobs that required a degree, or jobs in government.

Ideally, you should have both.

It was about reputation as much as stability. Good jobs made for status-filled conversations at family gatherings. They looked respectable, safe, and socially acceptable.

And while I did end up in both categories, I can't claim it was the result of great strategy; I certainly wasn't actively lining up the chess pieces. It just happened. But I can see now how much those childhood ideals quietly shaped where I landed. They made it easy to choose what looked right, even when it didn't feel right.

As I have grown in my career and followed my own path, I haven't made any wild, rule-breaking choices yet. No dramatic career change, no dropping everything to move overseas.

But maybe freedom doesn't always look like burning it all down.

In that very first role, the one in which I stayed too long, I wore my exhaustion like a badge of honour. Ten years in the same role; I told myself I was lucky, that this was what good and responsible adults did.

But luck can look a lot like quiet misery when you're running on autopilot.

And when burnout hit, it hit hard.

I had nothing left to give.

Not to my work.

Not to anyone.

Not even to myself.

It was a massive freaking wake-up call.

I left, eventually. I walked away from the job that had eaten so much of my time and energy.

I landed in a new role, still solid, still secure, but this one didn't drain me. It felt like exhaling after holding my breath for years.

Now, I earn comfortably, and I am proud of that. But I've stopped seeing money as proof that I am enough.

My value isn't tied to my job title or my salary anymore.

Success, to me, is being able to enjoy my life without constantly checking the clock or my bank balance.

If you'd asked me ten years ago what success meant, I'd have said: house, marriage, career, kids.

The checklist version.

The gleaming, lustrous package, which looks neat from a distance.

Now?

Success looks like balance.

Success is waking up without dread.

Success is surrounding myself with people who make me feel good and giving my energy to things that matter. It is a comfortable, happy life, one that I have built on purpose, to suit me.

There's nothing wrong with wanting a simple, steady life if that is your dream.

But please, let it be *your* dream.

The Mirror I Didn't Choose

From as far back as I can remember, my body was never just mine.

It was compared, commented on, and measured, especially by family. My grandparents meant well, but they would always compare my body to that of my sister or cousins. They would say my 'eight' instead of my 'weight,' as if it were an identity rather than a number.

Those small comments stick like chewing gum on the sole of a shoe, impossible to get off.

You internalise them without knowing it.

In my late twenties, after my divorce, those voices grew louder. I started believing I wouldn't find love again if I didn't fit some imaginary standard: smaller, thinner, more desirable.

There was no way I could find a new partner if I were curvy.

That thinking spiralled, and I developed an eating disorder.

It wasn't about food; it was about control.

Fuck the Fairytale: Find Your Own Magic

Everything else in my life felt chaotic, but this? This I could manage.

Until I couldn't.

It took a health scare and a hard conversation with my mum, her eyes full of fear, for me to really see what I was doing.

It broke me open.

I sought professional help.

Slowly, painfully, I rebuilt my relationship with my body.

I won't romanticise it. Some days I still struggle. But now I see my body as an ally, not an enemy. It carries me through life, through heartbreak, joy, exhaustion, and laughter.

My body deserves more than punishment.

The fairytale never warned us about the years we'd spend trying to unlearn the damage of trying to look enough.

My body has been through a war, not the kind people see, but the kind that happens quietly, behind locked doors.

Recovery wasn't linear. It was messy, imperfect, and full of setbacks. But each time I got back up, I trusted myself a little more.

Being resilient doesn't mean bouncing back without a scratch; it means knowing you can stand again, even if the effort leaves you marked and worn.

Now, I try to treat my body with respect.

Nourish it.

Move it.

Let it rest.

My body isn't perfect, but neither am I.

And that's the whole point.

Mandy Merrifield

The Good Woman Blueprint

Being a good woman was always the expectation.

A good daughter.

A good partner.

A good friend.

And for the most part, I've been lucky. I have a mum and sister who modelled what that looked like in healthy ways. They taught me that being good isn't about being obedient.

It is about being kind, loyal, and respectful, without losing yourself in the process.

But I've veered off that path a few times. I've stayed in relationships too long and shrunk myself to keep the peace.

I have put other people's needs so far ahead of my own that I couldn't see where I ended and they began.

The cost of being good was often silence; I wouldn't speak up when something didn't feel right.

I'm learning that sometimes, being a good woman means disappointing people.

Saying no.

Walking away.

Drawing lines.

It's still goodness, just not the kind that gets applause.

My family never punished me for choosing differently. They supported me through my divorce, through career changes, and through the messy middle. They've always loved me without the condition of compliance.

That kind of acceptance is rare, and I don't take it for granted.

I've learned that holding love for your family while living differently is a balancing act. You can honour where you came from without letting it define where you're going.

Over time, I've learned to curate my circle, gently but intentionally.

Some relationships faded because they no longer aligned with who I was becoming. Others ended abruptly because I finally recognised what didn't feel safe.

The people in my life now?

They are walking sunshine.

Supportive.

Honest.

Kind.

They see me, the real me. Not the version I thought I was supposed to be. They make space for my growth and remind me that it's okay to be both strong and soft.

They are the real magic in my world.

The Magic

I wasn't raised in a particularly spiritual or religious household. Faith wasn't a major influence in my story.

But connection, that is where I find meaning.

My magic comes from people.

My family, my friends, my partner. Colleagues who have become like family. They are my grounding force.

I find my sacred moments in sunlight, in conversations that stretch late into the night, in laughter that heals old wounds.

Maybe that's all spirituality really is: the quiet sense that you are part of something bigger, built from love, trust, and truth.

Leaving my relationships, both of them, was the bravest thing I've done. They were stable, respectable, and familiar. But they weren't true.

Finding freedom and magic on the other side wasn't simple.

It was messy, like a rollercoaster.

Highs that felt euphoric, and lows that knocked the wind out of me.

There were adventures: new countries, new people, a version of myself that finally felt alive.

But there was also guilt, self-doubt, and health struggles.

That's the part people don't tell you: the search for freedom and magic can come with a cost.

It is a price worth paying.

The fairytale tells us life should follow one neat, linear path: marriage, kids, money. When our life doesn't follow that straight line, it begs the question: Have you failed? Was the cost too high? What if the magic is just an illusion?

But what if the detours are the point?

Looking back on my life now, I feel a sense of quiet pride.

Not because I have it all figured out. I don't. But because I've built a life that feels mine.

I've learned that happiness isn't loud. It is not the highlight reel. It is slow mornings, coffee in hand, sunshine on your skin, people who make you laugh, and work that doesn't drain your soul.

It is knowing you can rely on yourself.

It is choosing peace over performance.

It is understanding that freedom is the dream.

I don't know exactly what is next for me, and I don't know where that freedom will take me, and that's the beauty of it.

For the first time, I'm not chasing a checklist.

I'm not measuring my worth by how close I am to someone else's version of happily ever after.

Freedom, for me, isn't about being wild or reckless. It is about being honest.

Freedom is saying, "This is who I am. This is what I want. And that is enough."

Maybe one day I'll have kids.

Maybe I won't.

Maybe I'll change careers again or move somewhere new.

But whatever comes next, it will be mine.

Because while the fairytale taught me how to please everyone, freedom taught me how to belong to myself.

And that's where I'm heading now, towards a life that feels like home, even if it doesn't look like anyone else's idea of perfect.

Mandy Merrifield

A love letter to my younger self

Don't dwell on what people think of you too much; focus more on what you feel about yourself.

At the end of the day, if you aren't happy with who you are, you can't share your love with those around you.

It won't be easy, and you will have some really dark moments, but everything will work out in the end, I promise.

Me x

Sophia: Pause, Breath

Growing up, I learned that love means hurt.

Staying quiet was normal.

Don't upset anyone.

Forgiveness fixes everything.

Being 'too much' might cost you love.

I carried these lessons like shadows that didn't fade, even after the sun went down. I believed it was noble to absorb pain without complaint. I thought being kind meant accepting the unacceptable, and that if someone was loving but also cruel, then at least they loved you.

Right?

And surely, because they said they loved you, that meant you should disregard the cruelty that came along for the ride.

Right?

While I now know this is wrong, I didn't know it at the time. And so, I silenced pieces of myself that wanted to speak up or take up space.

I gave without boundaries, believing that being good meant not being loud, not being seen, not asking for more.

I remember sitting on the edge of my bed as a teenager, pretending the music was blocking out the tension in the house. I turned up the music, hoping the volume would quieten the noise of the pressure I felt.

I wanted to scream, to tell someone how unfair it all felt. I wanted to talk openly about what I was going through and the pressure I felt. I was having a really tough time at school, and I had no one to talk to; my mum was busy with my younger siblings, and my dad was always at work. Every single day was hard, but I pretended that I was fine.

Words carried consequences. I did not feel safe enough to trust anyone.

Safety at a young age comes from your parents, and that was not an environment my mum and dad built for me. I was so scared of letting them down, even something small like failing a test, they would be so mad! The fear I felt at the anger I thought would come sat heavy in my head and in my body. How could I tell them everything I had going on? Surely if I did, my whole world would crumble.

The thought of sharing anything personal, let alone my deepest feelings, was overwhelming, and so I stayed quiet. I remember Mum asked me once what was going on, and because I didn't feel she was on my side, I stayed mute.

I tucked my voice into a corner and left the words there, and I told myself that it didn't matter.

My small hands learned that silence could protect me, even if it meant sacrificing pieces of my heart.

There's a subtle, almost invisible training in this, a conditioning that tells you, without saying a word, that your feelings are secondary.

Your voice is negotiable.

Your needs are optional.

Growing up and entering my teenage years, I started shrinking myself quietly, piece by piece, hiding parts of me, hoping to fit into the narrow space carved out for me. It felt like the right thing to do, and I always wanted to do the right thing: 'be a good daughter, don't disappoint.'

For years, I succeeded. I was good, polite, and manageable. But that kind of success comes with a cost.

You lose touch with who you are.

Pause. Breathe. Acknowledge that even surviving quietly required courage.

When the Mirror Shatters

The fairytale cracked the day I woke up emotionally, fully awake, and realised that what I thought was love was something else entirely.

It happened in my marriage.

Fuck the Fairytale: Find Your Own Magic

Watching my partner's rage spill over onto our child was like watching a mirror shatter; something deep inside me knew this wasn't love. In my mind's eye, I saw my mother and I saw my six-year-old self: my dad was mad at me, and rather than protecting me, she said nothing.

This image, from so many years ago, was like an out-of-body experience repeating itself in the present. The scream that unleashed from my body was so loud it deafened my own ears. It came from a space deep inside, one that I did not even know was there. All I knew in that moment was that I did not want to be my mother, I wanted to stand up for my daughter. And simultaneously, with that scream, my marriage shattered into a million pieces.

We had been so in love when we met, and as the scream released from my body, and as I saw my marriage break in that instant, I also saw a carousel of memories starting from the very first day we had fallen in love.

The scream was enough to stop his rage, and I am so thankful for that.

I knew that no more could I allow control to disguise itself as care; I had been blind to it for too long. I knew the pattern had to stop with me. Standing in the doorway, my daughter clutching her blanket, my responsibility was clear. I needed to protect my daughter and myself at the same time. Because that is what love is.

I had spent years rationalising, excusing, forgiving.

I thought love meant patience, endurance, and hope. But tolerance wasn't love. And that realisation hit me like a spiritual earthquake.

It was disorienting and terrifying.

Everything I had known about love, marriage, and family felt wrong. I had been performing, bending myself to fit a story that never matched reality. And I had been paying the price in pieces of my own heart.

Pause. Feel the weight of recognising that the world you believed in was not as it seemed.

Mandy Merrifield

Choosing Me

The fairytale never fit.

Not really.

And I tried, over and over, to make it fit.

I shrank myself.

I whispered my desires.

I muted my laughter.

I tried to be the version of me that would be acceptable, the version that would be chosen.

But one day, I realised that being chosen for my quietness, my compliance, or my smallness wasn't love.

It was the acceptance of convenience.

I wanted more.

I wanted to choose myself.

Not in arrogance or rebellion, but in clarity. I wanted to wake up to my own truth and live it unapologetically. It wasn't easy.

I felt so alone.

I did not know how to ask for help, and I wasn't even sure whether I was worthy of it.

It felt like abandoning a map I had carried for decades, one that told me which roads were safe and which were forbidden. But I needed to walk without a map.

I needed to trust my instincts, my heart, my own awareness of right and wrong.

Some mornings, I woke with heaviness in my chest, questioning if I could really do it, if I could live fully awake. But the alternative was no longer acceptable. I could no longer shrink, quiet, or vanish into a script that wasn't mine.

Fuck the Fairytale: Find Your Own Magic

Therapy. Evolution. A marriage reimagined.

Pause. Recognise the bravery in standing up for yourself, even when the ground shakes beneath your feet.

For years, I lived with emotional dissonance, smiling on the outside while building entire worlds inside my mind just to stay afloat.

Pretending I was okay when inside I was cracking.

I stopped sharing with my parents.

I stopped believing my voice mattered.

I stopped expecting my truth to be seen.

The first cracks of freedom came in the form of connection, real, honest connection. A friend suggested I start meditating, and so I did. Meditation gave me peace, and it gave me clarity. It allowed me to elevate to a new level of consciousness, a new level of awareness of what I wanted my world and my life to look like.

Conversations that made me feel heard. Creating my podcast became my act of rebellion, my reclamation. It was a space where I could be fully seen, where my thoughts, my pain, my contradictions were valid. Through it, I found women who understood me, who resonated with my experience, who reminded me that I wasn't broken, I was becoming.

I remember a conversation early on, talking with a woman I barely knew but who had been through her own version of heartbreak and awakening. She said, "You're not wrong for feeling what you feel. You're not too sensitive or too loud or too much. You're human."

Hearing that was like exhaling for the first time in years.

Connection isn't about agreement; it is about recognition and seeing each other fully.

That recognition gave me the courage to stop shrinking.

Pause. Let the truth of being seen sink in. The world feels lighter when you are recognised.

Mandy Merrifield

Love, Untamed

I was taught that love meant making it work no matter what. Leaving my marriage was a betrayal, and it was selfish. This wasn't just about me anymore.

Perhaps my ego also played a part? Perhaps I did not want to be seen as a failure?

Especially when I had committed with the best of intentions. I carried that belief like a compass through my marriage, trying to hold together something fractured.

Until one day, I realised: love without respect isn't love. It is minimising yourself to a point of suppression, erasure.

After the rage incident with my daughter, I stayed. Are you surprised?

I think looking back, I probably am too.

At the time, I stayed because of the story I told myself: my parents wouldn't understand, my daughter needed stability, and if I tried harder, maybe things would repair. But deep down, the marriage had already dissolved. I felt lost, numb, and I was aching for connection.

During that period, I grew close to someone I worked with online. The connection made me feel understood and cared for, and through our conversations, I began learning, growing, and coming back to life.

In that vulnerable space, the emotional lines blurred.

Then one day, everything surfaced.

My husband saw us talking on the phone and realised how close we had become. In that moment, the illusion my husband and I had been holding onto collapsed, showing us who we had each grown into, separately and together.

That rupture began a raw and uncomfortable awakening; the kind that forces you to face your fears, your truth, and what you want your life to stand for.

I'm not proud of how it happened, but I am proud of how I walked through the fire.

Therapy was the first step, and choosing to keep the family together wasn't easy, but it mattered.

In the aftermath, I leaned on gratitude and trusted God more than ever.

To be honest, even after therapy, I felt lost, yet somehow, I also felt found. It was as if I was slowly waking up; something was stirring inside, bringing me back to me.

I held myself up through the uncertainty, trusting that clarity would come.

Aligned love feels different.

It feels congruent.

It is still not perfect. No fairytale ending there, folks.

I'm still learning how to navigate marriage with more awareness and less illusion. It hasn't been a smooth or simple road, but it is one I choose every day. I feel grounded in my choice to love my husband and my family consciously.

Who I am inside matches my outside. It's not about pretending calm or performing normalcy. It's being truthful, even when it's hard.

Aligned love respects your wellbeing.

You can't pour from an empty cup, and you can't keep allowing others to walk over your boundaries to keep the peace.

Real love, at its core, is self-loving. It nurtures your wholeness first, so you can truly nurture others.

I've learned to love myself differently now.

By tending to every part of me: body, mind, emotions.

By taking care of my soul and my spirit.

I move my body, train, study, keep learning.

I am aware of how emotions shape our wellbeing, how carrying negativity can manifest as illness or disconnection.

I love myself even when guilt or shame come calling.

Love now includes acceptance.

I have learned to love myself when I'm thriving and when I'm tender, raw, and still healing.

Pause. Let the possibility of loving yourself completely feel possible. Even when it's messy, it's still love.

Work That Breathes

Growing up, the 'appropriate' careers were safe, respectable, conservative, jobs that didn't ask you to be visible or expressive.

A good career was steady, modest, invisible.

Still, creativity pulled at me, persistently.

I found a compromise, working behind the camera instead of in front. Directing, filming, designing, and media became my language, and storytelling became my craft.

A craft I excelled at. I was winning awards for my films, and I felt purposeful. All of the feelings and words that I had wanted to say, I now watched them leave the actors' mouths in the form of dialogue I had written. It felt so good to be seen and heard and understood. I was bringing untold stories to life through filmmaking. And I felt lighter.

Passion finds a way, even when it isn't welcomed with open arms.

After my second baby, I consciously defied expectations.

I left the predictable nine-to-five grind, choosing freedom over security.

I wanted to build work around my children's rhythms, create from home, nurture my soul.

My husband struggled to understand because stability looked like a paycheque to him.

To me, stability looked like inner peace.

Choosing coaching was about alignment, work that healed rather than drained, and work that reflected what I truly value: time, presence, energy.

It was terrifying and freeing.

Terrifying because I left behind what was considered secure.

Freeing because I was finally designing a life that matched who I was becoming.

Success now feels different.

Not titles or money, but presence.

Watching my children grow emotionally, responding calmly instead of reacting, learning and evolving, these moments are my markers of success. I release outcomes that aren't aligned, no longer measure worth by productivity, and find peace in flowing with life rather than forcing it.

Pause. Notice how work can be a form of liberation, not just survival.

Owning My Skin

As with most teenagers, the tween years delivered many changes in my body. I had the classic zits-and-braces face, and so confidence was not something I had in spades.

While I was taught to speak softly, to avoid attention, and to make sure I didn't laugh too loudly, I have to say, I didn't care too much. Honestly, the lack of confidence made it convenient. And so I lived the lessons well.

As my body began to change, suddenly every movement felt scrutinised, and every impulse dangerous. While I thought nothing of my body, and while I believed I was definitely less than ordinary, along came a boy. And he said he loved me. I wanted to feel pretty, and I wanted to feel wanted, and so I was ready to do anything for him. That, in the end, led to a deep trauma.

After years of inner work, childbirth, and healing, I was able to reclaim my body.

I now speak to her, listen to her, and nurture her.

My body is not an object anymore; she is my living, breathing companion.

At eighteen, trauma made me disconnect completely.

I carried shame and guilt instead of trust.

There were moments I wanted to give up entirely, but in my darkest teenage hours, something, a voice in my head, I believe it was God's grace, kept me tethered to life and to hope. Rebuilding trust meant learning to feel safe in my skin again, to honour every scar.

The girl I was at eighteen was lost; the woman I am now is home in her body.

Pause. Breathe into the sensation of being present in your own skin.

Family Without Chains

I was taught a good woman stays quiet, sacrifices, obeys.

A good daughter, wife, mother, friend never challenges; she always gives, and is always kind.

I tried to live those versions, and I rebelled against them too.

Obedience cost me my voice, my full life.

Authenticity, eventually, became my power.

As the eldest of four, expectations shaped me early: be responsible, stay safe, avoid risks.

I split myself in two for decades: the version they wanted and the version I was becoming.

Learning to communicate with compassion but without compliance became essential.

Now, I honour both truths, theirs and mine, without taking their disapproval personally.

The family I've created now is home.

My children are my heart.

My podcast and coaching community are my tribe.

My trainer, Amanda, is one of my safe spaces; I can be unfiltered, raw, and heard. She helps me to know there is safety in being myself, and that I do not have to please everyone all of the time. The more I train with her, the safer I feel in my body. I am thankful that I choose to train, and I am thankful that I have the intuition to surround myself with people who lift me up.

Pause. Reflect on how belonging can be chosen, not only inherited.

God in the Ordinary

Faith has always been both a blessing and a struggle.

I grew up surrounded by intuitive, spiritual people.

My father taught me God is love and that the world itself is proof of divinity.

My perspective of Islam is gentle, compassionate, beautiful; it provides inner peace by connecting humanity through one heart.

At eighteen, trauma dimmed that light. I believed I was unworthy, punished myself with shame. Years later, I realised God never asked for perfection.

Grace is not earned; it exists in every moment, broken or radiant.

My relationship with the divine is Sufi-like, a flow between devotion, surrender, and love.

I find connection in stillness, barefoot, breathing, watching morning light, meditating.

Magic is the alchemy of thought into form, idea into creation, intention into reality.

We are all creators of our lives.

Pause. Consider that life itself can be a spiritual practice.

Awake and Becoming

I've walked away emotionally from conformity, pretending, staying small, even when physically present.

Freedom is clarity.

Living fully, loving deeply, moving without masks.

Happiness today is simple: my children's laughter, coaching, ordinary rituals of health and movement, expanding at forty-two.

Gratitude for growth, creation, and becoming, that is my fairytale now.

Not perfection, not compliance, but awake living, fully and fiercely.

Pause. Let the quiet certainty of becoming yourself settle deep inside.

A love letter to my younger self

My darling girl,

The whole world is waiting for you. You don't have to escape your reality to find peace or love; it already lives inside you. You are love, and you are loved more than you can ever imagine. Don't let the pain of feeling unseen convince you that you are invisible. What your relatives or friends can't reflect back to you right now doesn't define your worth. You are magic in motion.

Don't spend your youth trying to please or perform. Don't let fear of disappointment make you shrink. Follow your heart's wild ideas: sing, dance, create, act, express. You were never meant to be small. Education matters, but it's not the measure of your soul. You are beautiful, radiant, and whole, exactly as you are. Don't run from your feelings; let them become art, let them become your purpose. You will go through storms, but you will rise from every one happier, wiser, softer.

I love you truly, madly, deeply, and I'm so proud of the woman you'll become.

Chapter 7:
The Sex and the City Myth

The Gospel According to Carrie

If you were a woman in the 1990s or early 2000s, chances are *Sex and the City* wasn't just a TV show; it was a religion.

Carrie Bradshaw was our priestess, the column was her scripture, New York City was the holy land, and the lifestyle the four girls led was the holy grail we aspired to.

We gathered around our boxy TVs, martinis or cosmos in hand (let's be honest: it was probably cheap wine), and absorbed every sermon about love, friendship, and Manolos as if the words were sent from God herself.

And we believed in it.

With every fibre of our being.

The dream of being single and fabulous, of living an incredibly glamorous life of never-ending brunches, galleries, and parties, of being strong and independent, but still irresistible to men.

Because that was the real subtext: the power of the independent woman still hinged on who wanted her.

Charlotte: "I've been dating since I was 15, I'm exhausted. Where is he?"

You could be smart, successful, and stylish, but only if you were also great in bed, and, of course, eventually chosen.

It wasn't malicious.

It was seductive.

We wanted it.

Sex and the City was the first time women's messy inner lives were splashed across the screen without apology: the talking about sex, the friendships, the vibrators, the brunches.

Fuck the Fairytale: Find Your Own Magic

It was a revolution.

It was even banned in some countries.

When Singapore's Ministry of Information, Communication and Arts finally lifted the ban in 2004, they still censored scenes, particularly those featuring Kim Cattrall's Samantha, where she used sexually charged expletives or when she exposed her breasts.

Looking back now, it also feels like we were tricked into thinking that empowerment and outright hedonistic decadence were the same thing.

We were told freedom looked like shoes that cost a month's rent.

Independence meant being able to afford your own apartment, but still crying into your cosmo because Mr Big didn't call.

Having it all meant doing everything alone, and then numbing the loneliness with cocktails and credit card debt.

Carrie Bradshaw became both the dream and the crutch for women around the world.

She was complex, sure, but she was also chaos wrapped in couture.

The woman who couldn't pay her rent but bought Dior, Chanel, and Gucci.

The woman who said she was fine being single but unravelled every time a man pulled away.

Who remembers the Berger break-up? The post-it note: "I'm sorry. I can't. Don't hate me."

And then the absolute meltdown that followed?

The woman who thought writing about love meant she understood it.

And we, sitting there, cheap wine in hand, lapped it up.

We learned to romanticise dysfunction.

To believe that if someone actually showed a bit of gratitude for our presence (cue Big and his heart 'thing,' season 6: *The Domino Effect*), then all the gaslighting, uncertainty, and emotional whiplash were just part of the story.

It wasn't chaos; it was chemistry.

The Cult of Mr Big

Let's talk about him.

The tall, charming, emotionally unavailable archetype who ruined an entire generation's idea of what love should feel like. Mine included. I fight against it to this day.

Mr Big wasn't just a character; he was a masterclass in exactly the type of man who was toxic.

Gaslighting.

A situationship.

After Carrie discovers that Big is still happily dating other women, she muses:

"I wondered. In a city like New York, with its infinite possibilities, has monogamy become too much to expect?"

And just like that, we *did* expect that monogamy was too much to expect. We unknowingly, unwittingly, unconsciously, lowered our standards.

Love was meant to be hard.

We should be grateful for the breadcrumbs thrown our way by the handsome man. What more could we want? Weren't we lucky he even looked our way? That he chose us, even if it was only for that moment?

Big was the poster-child for every situationship, every slow-burning emotional hangover that left women in therapy convincing themselves it wasn't their fault he didn't choose them.

He taught us that emotional inconsistency was sexy.

That detachment was power.

That the best kind of love was one that kept you on your toes, preferably in Jimmy Choos.

And Carrie? She was complicit. She kept answering the phone. Kept turning up. Kept mistaking chemistry for compatibility.

And what did we see?

We didn't see boundaries; we saw persistence.

We didn't see trauma bonding; we saw true love.

Big wasn't the villain; he was the reward.

He got the final word, the final episode, the final say.

The man who couldn't commit for six seasons became the one she married in the end.

And you know what? That was the ultimate betrayal; that final ending.

Carrie ending up in her 'happily ever after' with Mr Big went against everything the show supposedly stood for: the independent, empowered woman.

None of it mattered because she finally got her man.

Imagine if *Sex and the City* had ended differently.

"I don't live here anymore," she yells as she walks down Perry Street, on the way to her final dinner with the girls before moving to Paris.

If Carrie had walked away from Big and stayed away, if she had chosen herself without needing him to see her worth, if the moral wasn't love conquers all…

That fairytale wouldn't have sold.

The public outcry would have been heard around the world.

And so, we absorbed the myth.

That if we're patient enough, forgiving enough, interesting enough, stylish enough, the emotionally unavailable man will eventually see what he has lost and come running back.

We built our romantic resilience on that lie.

We called it hope.

But was it?

The Chase, The Date, The Damn Validation

Somewhere between Carrie's monologues and Samantha's orgasmic moans, we got the message: the most important storyline in a woman's life was who she was dating.

Every brunch conversation circled back to a man.

Every plotline revolved around love, or the absence of it.

We were watching women who were supposed to have it all: careers, apartments, friendships, freedom; but somehow the show's gravity always pulled us back into the central orbit, and that orbit revolved around men.

Sex and the City told us we were allowed to want sex. Yes, but only in pursuit of love… well, maybe not in Samantha's case.

And even she ended up with her dream man.

We thought we were watching a revolution, women talking openly about desire. But it was still a revolution fought on male terrain.

The goal wasn't pleasure; it was approval.

Even for Samantha, whilst the goal might not have been approval in the sense of a relationship, it was definitely approval of her body, validation of her independent, strong career woman status, and admiration of her liberal approach to sex.

We learned to chase.

The show made singlehood look sparkly, but underneath, there was a quiet hum of panic.

The ticking clock. The brunch-table confessions that, no matter how glamorous, sophisticated or witty, still reeked of desperation.

We didn't see women just being.

We saw women perpetually waiting to be chosen and waiting to be loved.

Even their independence was temporary, a placeholder until the next man arrived to give the story momentum.

The Credit Card Cinderella Story

Here's what *Sex and the City* really sold us: not just love as validation, but lifestyle as identity.

Carrie Bradshaw couldn't afford her life.

She was a freelance columnist who somehow managed to live alone in a Manhattan brownstone, brunch like it was a full-time job, and spend obscene amounts of money on shoes; yet she rarely seemed to work.

It was fantasy economics dressed up as empowerment.

Independence looked like swiping your card for another pair of Manolos.

But what it normalised was debt.

It turned financial irresponsibility into a personality trait.

Carrie's financial fragility taught us that spending equals freedom. That retail therapy is empowerment. That being taken care of, whether emotionally or financially, is a perk of being fabulous.

The show never taught financial literacy.

Who could forget Carrie's math lesson from the pregnant Miranda?

"100 x $400? That's $40,000," says Miranda, "that's your down payment."

"I am going to be the old woman who lives in her shoes," quips Carrie.

And we listened. We didn't shake our heads in disbelief. We simply accepted that this was okay.

Real security was invisible, unless you were lucky enough to have Mr Big write you a cheque.

Which he did. And he saved her.

Fairytale much?

That quiet lesson shaped a generation.

We grew up thinking financial autonomy was optional, emotional dependence was romantic, and having it all meant putting on a show rather than achieving actual financial reality.

The Friendship Fantasy

Then there was the group.

The perfect, always-there-for-you, emotionally intuitive, brunch-ready group of best friends.

Carrie, Miranda, Charlotte, Samantha, wildly different women, yet perfectly aligned in schedules, emotional availability, and loyalty.

We watched and thought: this is what female friendship is supposed to be.

But real life isn't a TV montage.

Friends move, jobs demand, babies arrive, burnout happens. People aren't always available, understanding, or endlessly forgiving.

People change and grow apart.

It has happened to me, and it hurt. And it has probably happened to you too, my darling reader.

The work bestie: once you move to a different role or company, the closeness and everyday conversations fade.

The school clique: once upon a time, your 'ride-or-die' girl gang, they develop other interests, make new friends, and spend weekends with people you don't know.

Or you realise that once you've left school or changed jobs, you don't have much in common anymore.

It can be hard.

And sometimes friendships fade into the background, with the love and memories still intact. Sometimes they end abruptly, with harsh words and criticisms that once uttered, can never be repaired.

Sex and the City created a benchmark for friendship that was impossible, one that made women feel lonely if their own lives didn't match up. We internalised that true friendship must be constant, perfect, and selfless.

Real friendship isn't about being there for everything. It's about depth, trust, and presence, not curated brunches and moral support on demand.

A lesson I've learned along the way, and I absolutely cannot take credit for this one: people come into your life for a reason, a season, or a lifetime.

Google it.

It makes so much sense.

The Hangover

I'm lucky; I don't have hangovers anymore. Not the ones you're thinking of anyway.

But what about the emotional hangover?

The hangover we get when we've built our life around a myth.

When you've spent your twenties and thirties chasing the version of womanhood you were told was aspirational, only to find yourself burnt out, disconnected, and disappointed.

You wake up and see that *Sex and the City* didn't teach us how to be free.

It taught us to wait, to be chosen, and to accept the bare minimum.

We mistook chaos for aliveness.

Availability for intimacy.

Being rescued for being loved.

Appearances for achievement.

The show didn't just mess with our love lives. It messed with how we live.

Where To From Here

We can still love what *Sex and the City* gave us: the friendship, the honesty, the permission to talk about things our mothers couldn't.

But we can also hold it accountable for what it cost us.

We can stop chasing the unrealistic fantasy that the four women delivered to our screens and lives, and instead start choosing a reality a little closer to home.

It probably won't be as dazzling as the bright lights of New York City, but it will give you comfort in your own skin.

How the Generations see Sex and the City

Alright, let's talk about what women today actually think of *Sex and the City*, because the myth has aged, not gracefully.

And give me some creative licence here, I might make some sweeping statements.

Forgive me if they don't apply to all of you, my darling readers.

Millennials and late Gen X (like me) grew up on it. They remember the fashion, the New York skyline, the cocktails, the brunches. It was a sacred rite of passage.

And yes, we absorbed the whole Carrie and Mr Big blueprint.

We chased emotionally unavailable guys, analysed every text, obsessed over men who barely noticed us, and somehow believed our worth was measured by how many shoes we could buy on a newspaper columnist's salary.

Are you a millennial? How do you reflect on this now?

Can you look back and laugh at the late-night tears over some guy who ghosted you, or the endless 'maybe if I try harder he'll call' energy you embodied?

Or does the hangover still linger, the quiet worry about being enough, or the sneaky pressure to perform as if your life is a highlight reel?

Gen Z? They didn't grow up with it, but they've seen clips, TikToks, and memes.

They can be merciless.

Carrie's drama? Eye-roll city.

Samantha's over-the-top confidence? A lesson in 'don't be that extra'.

Charlotte's hopeless romanticism? Laughable.

And Mr Big? Forget it, he's a case study in emotional unavailability.

Gen Z sees the show for what it is: a cautionary tale.

They aren't taking notes on how to get a man; they're taking screenshots for memes, and that's probably the healthiest way to consume this show. It is entertainment, nothing more.

Early Gen X watched it as adults.

For the most part, they were already juggling work, relationships, maybe kids. They saw through the glitter fast.

These women got the humour, the dialogue, the cheeky feminist sheen, but they knew it was a fantasy. Brunches, friendships, ridiculous shoe budgets, it wasn't real life.

They enjoyed *Sex in the City*, but it didn't dictate how they lived day to day.

Here's the thing though: across all generations, the messaging about men was the same.

Big was emotionally unavailable and selfish; yet the show sold him as the ultimate prize.

And that's the kicker: so many of us learned that male attention equals validation.

And while the platforms may have changed, the attention-seeking is still there, only now it's DMs, swipes, likes, TikTok hearts.

The myth is alive and well.

Are there lessons to be had?

Perhaps.

Here is one thing for sure: *Sex and the City* didn't just entertain us; in the 1990s and early 2000s, it quietly rewired how women measure themselves, their relationships, and even their friendships.

And the hangover continues today.

Find Your Own Magic: A Guided Reflection

Unpacking the Mr Big Myth

I have chased my version of Mr Big for most of my adult life.

The suit, the power, the dominance.

The unavailability. Waiting for the phone to ring. Forgiving and making excuses for them when the text message doesn't arrive.

The casual trysts, hoping it would turn into more. The situationships. The breadcrumbing.

I've accepted it all.

Because I wanted *my* Mr Big.

What a tough lesson to unlearn.

I'm on my way, but I still have a long way to go. Shall we do this one together?

Step 1: Identify the Narrative You Absorbed

Think back to your formative years. Remember *Sex and the City*? The brunches, the Manolos, the heartbreak, the constant chase.

Ask yourself:

- What messages about men did I take from that show?

- Did it teach me that men should always be emotionally unavailable?

- Did it make me believe that the more difficult a man is to get, the more desirable he is?

- Did I learn that persistence in chasing a man equals proof of love?

Write it all down. Be honest. No censoring.

(Note from me: relationships come in all shapes, sizes, genders, and preferences. Feel free to swap the word "men" for whatever fits your experience.)

Step 2: Separate Myth from Reality

Now, reflect on your own relationships, crushes, or dating experiences.

- Which of those messages turned out to be true?

- Which were complete myths?

- How many times have you chased someone who didn't see your value, because you were unconsciously following the Mr Big blueprint?

Be specific. List patterns, moments, or feelings you now recognise as learned behaviours from media rather than your authentic instincts.

Step 3: Examine Your Beliefs About Men

Now, dig a little deeper:

- Do I expect men to validate my worth?

- Do I believe a man's attention equals love or security?

- Do I excuse bad behaviour because he's complicated, or it's part of the story, or 'just who he is '?

- How has chasing someone affected my self-respect or happiness?

Write freely. This exercise is about awareness, not judgment.

Step 4: Reframe the Story

Now that you've identified the patterns, rewrite the script. Ask yourself:

- What do I actually want from men? Not from the show, society, or the cultural myth, but from a real connection?

- What behaviours, values, and actions would feel safe, respectful, and mutually supportive?

- How can I stop confusing attention with love?

- What boundaries do I need to enforce to protect my emotional wellbeing?

Write your answers in the present tense, claiming them for yourself:

- I choose men who communicate clearly and consistently.

- I no longer chase attention that doesn't feel mutual.

- I value respect, honesty, and emotional availability over drama and allure.

Step 5: Action Step

Finally, take one small action to live this new narrative. Examples:

- Pause before replying to a text or DM. Ask if this interaction aligns with your values.

- Journal about a recent situation where you felt yourself chasing energy, and reframe it according to your new rules.

- Practice saying no or walking away from attention that doesn't feel reciprocal.

Mandy Merrifield

Kyles: The Value of Me

Me. Today.

A woman who is both soft and strong, someone who knows her worth, leads with her values, and lives with intention.

I am, at my core, a grateful person.

Grounded. Joyful. Curious.

Beauty comes in ordinary moments.

A morning coffee shared in stillness, the laughter of friends, the quiet satisfaction that comes from living in alignment with who I truly am. My life isn't about chasing perfection or performing for approval anymore; it's about presence, contribution, and meaning.

I speak up when it matters.

My compass points are not north, south, east or west; they are loyalty, kindness, and honesty.

These values steady me and guide how I move through the world.

Am I direct? Yes.

I have learned that truth delivered with care is one of the deepest forms of respect.

I work to live, not live to work. I make time for joy, for travel, for experiences that expand perspective and nourish the soul.

Is this indulgence?

No.

It is leadership of thyself.

Growing up in a small country town, I inherited a simple script for life: study hard, get a job, buy a home, have children. The elements of this script were not presented as options or questions to consider; they were a sequence, a path everyone was expected to follow. At the heart of the home was my Mum, and my Dad was the provider. Life was predictable, familiar, and in many ways safe. I was a shy girl, observant, sensitive, deeply connected to my family, and I took comfort in the sense of belonging.

But as I grew older, I began to feel the quiet tug of something beyond the boundary of what was expected.

I didn't have the language for it then, but looking back, it was the early stirrings of finding myself; the part of me that would later learn to question, to choose, and to define success in my own way. Moving to the city was the first real chapter break in the fairytale story I had been handed.

As the chapters slowly started to take shape, I realised, often the hard way, that life isn't a script to follow; it is a journey you create along the way.

That single understanding changed everything.

The fairytale, as uplifting as it once seemed, the ease of the path that had been presented to me as a given, began to unravel as I faced one of life's deepest reckonings: being told that I would not have children.

It is an experience that shakes not just your plans but calls into question your very sense of identity.

For a long time, I sat with the question: Who am I, if not a mother?

Society doesn't always make space for that question.

The narrative we are sold ties womanhood so tightly to motherhood that stepping outside of it can feel like exile. But in that loss, something remarkable began to take shape. My husband and I were forced to redefine what home meant and what love meant, without the expectation of children. It was agonising, yes, but also clarifying.

Love is not measured in milestones.

Big lesson.

It is found in the quiet courage of two people choosing each other, day after day, through grief, growth, and change.

Looking back now, I see that chapter not as an ending, but as a transformation.

The fairytale didn't fit because it was never mine to begin with.

My life didn't need to be rescued or rewritten; it needed to be reclaimed. In doing so, I found a kind of peace that only comes from living your truth, even when that truth diverges from what others expect.

That understanding, that we each have the power to define the shape of our own lives, has guided me ever since.

I have learned that self-leadership begins with awareness: of your values, your boundaries, and the patterns that no longer serve you.

For me, one of those patterns was the subtle expectation of being the one to compromise.

In family dynamics, I often found myself cast as the flexible one: the one who could adjust, travel, rearrange, and make it work. It took time to recognise how much energy that pattern consumed, and how often it left me feeling unseen.

In the past, I would yield to keep the peace, to hold on to connection, and to not rock the boat. But over time, I have learned that peace built on silence isn't peace at all; it is suppression.

True peace comes from living honestly, speaking your truth with respect, and standing firm in your boundaries.

That shift, from pleasing to leading, has been one of the most powerful lessons of my adult life.

Has this lesson come at a cost?

Yes.

Sometimes, standing in integrity has meant being left out, misunderstood, or judged.

I have come to understand that those moments are not evidence of failure; they are markers of growth. They remind me that fairness matters, and that leading yourself sometimes means standing alone for a while.

My beliefs around love and partnership have evolved just as deeply.

I was raised in an era and by a generation that equated a good marriage with endurance.

You stayed, no matter what.

You worked through it, you compromised, you carried on.

But endurance is not the same as love.

Love, as I see it now, is not about control or sacrifice without reciprocity. It is not silence for the sake of comfort, or shrinking to keep the peace. It is not earned by being useful, agreeable, or compliant.

Real love is spacious.

Real love allows you to grow.

Real love makes room for honesty, even when that honesty is uncomfortable.

Real love is both anchor and independence, a partnership built on respect, mutual effort, and truth.

It is choosing each other freely, not out of obligation or image, but out of a deep alignment of values.

Self-love, too, has changed shape over the years. It is no longer about accomplishing or proving; it is about nurturing.

Self-love means knowing when to pause.

It looks like moving my body, nourishing it well, wearing clothes that make me feel strong and confident, booking a relaxing massage without guilt, a trip to the hair salon, and, very simply, creating space for quiet.

Even a day spent guilt-free binge-watching trashy TV.

It is giving myself permission to enjoy, to travel, to rest, to laugh without justification.

Most importantly, it is forgiving myself when I fall short.

Forever my harshest critic, I have come to understand that discipline without compassion is just self-punishment.

True growth happens when you lead yourself gently, hold yourself accountable, and do both with grace held lightly to your heart.

I think back often to that young woman who once believed that success meant fitting in, ticking the right boxes, meeting the right expectations, and being liked.

She worked hard, achieved much, and still wondered if she was enough.

I wish I could tell her what I know now: 'enoughness' is not something you earn; it is something you embody when you finally stop performing.

Life has taught me that the most powerful kind of leadership is the one you practice within yourself.

A steady, daily act of aligning your actions with your values, your words with your truth, your choices with what really matters.

This is the work of a lifetime, and I am grateful every day to do it.

Redefining Love, Success, and Self

As I grew into myself, my understanding of love expanded far beyond the boundaries of romance or obligation.

Love, I have come to understand, is the practice of truth.

It is being able to look someone in the eye, especially yourself, and say, "This is who I am," without fear or performance.

Love is found in the quiet acts of consistency: showing up when it matters, offering presence rather than solutions, speaking honestly even when silence would be easier.

Fuck the Fairytale: Find Your Own Magic

It took time to learn that love isn't perfect.

Love is not a constant state of harmony or effortless connection.

Love is a living thing, sometimes messy, sometimes miraculous, and it thrives only when both people are willing to grow.

To me, love now looks like partnership in its purest sense: respect in disagreement, support without condition, laughter in the ordinary, and patience in the uncertain. It certainly isn't endless grand gestures or public declarations; it is the steady, private rhythm of two people choosing each other again and again.

And love of self, that is where leadership begins.

For years, I believed that being selfless was the highest form of love. I was taught that being good meant saying yes, smoothing over discomfort, and being everything for everyone. It took decades to unlearn that. Now I understand that love without boundaries is not love at all; it is self-erasure.

Self-love has become my anchor.

Self-love is not loud or performative; it is deliberate and quiet.

It is found in how I speak to myself on hard days, how I rest when my body asks, how I forgive when I fall short, and how I honour my truth even when it is inconvenient.

Self-leadership and self-love are, to me, inseparable.

Leading yourself means treating yourself with the same respect, patience, and compassion you would extend to someone you deeply care for.

My relationship with success has transformed just as profoundly.

In that fairytale, the one I was handed in that small country town, success was often defined by stability: a good job, a home, the visible markers of having made it.

In my family, money wasn't abundant, but we had what mattered: love, humour, flexibility, and a strong work ethic. We were taught that effort was honourable and contribution was more important than competition. These foundation stones shape who I am today.

Over the years, I have built a life that reflects both gratitude for where I came from and pride in how far I have come.

With a partnership grounded in equality, my husband and I have, through shared effort, shared values, and shared respect, created a bond so strong, so unshakeable, so enduring.

Nothing can or will break it.

We have faced the biggest challenges that could have easily broken us; instead, these have become the crucible that strengthened us into invincibility.

I look at what we have built, not the house, or the travels, or the outward signs of success, but the feeling of our life together.

And I am proud.

Proud of the work it took, proud of the lessons learned, and proud of the woman I became along the way.

There have been moments, of course, where I have absolutely felt judged.

I work hard and play hard. I have a nice bike, a beautiful home, we travel overseas and, yes, I own several Louis Vuittons.

But none of these things make me better than anyone else. I am not in competition with anyone. Unfortunately, that is not always how others see me.

The labels people place on you when they don't understand your story: lucky, spoiled, a silver spoon kid.

The truth is, I come from very modest beginnings and have worked my arse off to become who I am today.

So, to all the judgments, fuck them.

Judge all you want.

I know exactly who I am and how I got here.

Fuck the Fairytale: Find Your Own Magic

I have been told I have it easy because I don't have children.

Can you even imagine what that feels like?

I have been underestimated and, at times, envied even. But those opinions no longer sting the way they once did. I know who I am, and I know what it has taken to stand here today: the grit, the setbacks, the relentless work of becoming me.

I am so proud of my drive, my resilience, and the courage it takes to live authentically.

And yet, I've learned that strength isn't about being unshakeable; it is about staying open-hearted in a world that can so easily harden you. The more I lead myself, the more I realise that gratitude and power can coexist. You can be grounded in humility and still stand tall in your worth.

There was a time in my career when doing the right thing came with real cost. I witnessed something unjust, behaviour that was unethical and harmful, and every instinct in me screamed that silence would make me complicit. I could have looked the other way, as many do.

Values, once truly lived, don't allow for quiet comfort at the expense of integrity.

A colleague warned me, "Don't fall on your sword for this. It's not worth your job."

But to me, the real risk was in losing myself, and speaking up came with consequences: professional, emotional, and psychological.

It tested everything I believed about fairness and courage. But I stood my ground. And eventually, the truth surfaced, as it always does.

That experience changed me. It made me more empathetic, but also more discerning about where I place my energy. It reminded me that leadership is not about titles or applause; it is about integrity, doing what is right even when no one is watching, even when it costs you. I came out the other side bruised, but freer.

Unmistakable peace is the gift you give yourself when you don't betray yourself to fit in.

Success, for me now, is not defined by accolades or income.

Success is measured in alignment.

Success is how I feel when I wake in the morning, clear, grounded, content.

It is the balance between ambition and peace, achievement and rest. It is being able to move through life with an open heart and an uncluttered conscience.

As a woman, success means owning my voice without apology. It means using it to uplift others, to create space for truth, to model what self-trust looks like.

As a partner, success is a marriage that grows with us, where respect runs deeper than romance, and love evolves instead of eroding.

As a person, success means living in congruence with my values, even when no one notices but me.

I am still learning to let go of the need to be liked and the need to meet others' expectations. It is an ongoing practice, not a destination. But the more I lean into authenticity, the more I find peace. I have learned that when you surround yourself with people who share your values, there is no need for explanation; you are seen fully and freely for who you are.

In my younger years, I thought fulfilment was something you reached, a peak you arrived at once everything was in place. Now I know it is something to be cultivated over time, moment by moment, second by second, through each choice you make.

Success today feels quieter but deeper. It is in the way I respond, rather than react.

The way I listen.

The way I keep learning.

The way I hold space for others without losing myself.

And through all of it, the achievements, the setbacks, the rebuilding, I have worked out that growth isn't about becoming someone new.

It is about returning to who you have always been, before the world told you who you should be.

Every challenge has peeled back another layer, revealing not just resilience, but a deep, abiding sense of gratitude.

I am grateful for the lessons that have tested me along the way.

Grateful for the moments that required courage.

Grateful for the times I had to choose integrity over comfort.

Each one of these moments strengthened my sense of self and deepened my understanding of what it means to lead from within.

Leadership is not a role; it is a relationship.

With yourself.

With your truth.

With your impact on others.

And when that relationship is grounded in gratitude and guided by values, everything else begins to fall into place.

That, to me, is the heart of success.

Not flawlessness, but presence.

Not arrival, but alignment.

Not approval, but authenticity.

Peace

There is a quiet point you reach in life where you see that peace is no longer something you chase; it is something you curate.

It is not loud or dramatic; it is the slow exhale that comes when you finally make peace with who you are, where you have been, and where you are going.

For me, that peace arrived gradually, through the practice of integration, learning to hold all the parts of myself, not in competition, but in conversation.

Family is the first and hardest classroom for that kind of peace.

My family is full of love, complexity, and difference. A web of people doing their best with what they've been given. We have certainly had our share of misunderstandings, silences, and unspoken rules. For years, I thought harmony meant avoidance; that loving your family meant keeping the peace at any cost.

Now I understand that peace built on silence is fragile.

Real connection requires truth, even when it's uncomfortable.

I have learned to meet my family where they are, not where I wish they were.

I have learned to see their patterns without judgment, and so too my own, without defensiveness.

There is so much freedom in doing this, in accepting that you can love someone deeply and still need distance, boundaries, or space to breathe.

Maturity in action: I love you, and I need this for me.

No guilt.

Life-changing.

Over time, my definition of family has expanded beyond blood.

It includes the people who see me clearly, the friends who hold space for my joy and also for my struggle, and those who remind me of who I am when I forget.

The chosen family I have built around me over the years is one of my life's greatest blessings.

They are the ones who walk beside me without condition, celebrate my growth without envy, and understand that love doesn't need to be constantly on show to be certain.

Faith, too, has evolved.

I don't mean religion, though I honour those who find comfort there, but a deep, quiet faith in something larger than logic.

Faith that there is meaning in the unfolding, even when I can't see it yet.

Faith that the lessons will arrive at the right time.

Faith that every ending holds a beginning.

I no longer search for signs; I listen for alignment.

My faith now lives in the ordinary, in the way morning light touches the kitchen counter, in the sound of rain, in the rhythm of my breath when I run. I find divinity in small acts of presence, in moments that remind me how sacred it is just to be here.

Gratitude, I've learned, is a form of prayer.

There was a time when I pushed my body hard, as though achievement could outrun tiredness. I lived on adrenaline and ambition, convincing myself that rest was indulgence. It took a few scares and a few too many sleepless nights to come to terms with how deeply disconnected I had become from my own body's wisdom. I had to relearn how to listen, how to eat when hungry, rest when tired, and move for joy rather than punishment.

Now, I see my body as my oldest companion. It has carried me through grief and laughter, through long days and new beginnings.

My body deserves reverence, not criticism.

There is still a constant striving for balance, and I do the best I can.

I embrace movement that feels good, food that nourishes, and rest that restores.

I no longer chase perfection; I seek presence.

There is something profoundly healing in coming home to your own body after years of treating it like a project.

To stand in front of a mirror, unposed, and think: This is me. Alive. Capable. Enough.

That kind of acceptance can't be found in a reflection; it is cultivated in the way you inhabit yourself, day after day.

In work, in love, in health, I have learned that the truest form of power is calm.

Not the kind of calm that suppresses, but the kind that steadies. The kind that says, 'I can hold this,' even when life is messy or uncertain. It is a calm that comes from alignment, from knowing your values so deeply that they guide you through the noise.

And that is what integration feels like: when the different parts of your life stop competing and start harmonising. When your choices, relationships, and routines all start speaking the same language: the language of truth.

Legacy is a word I used to associate with grand gestures, the kind of thing left behind in buildings or books or family trees.

I have come to see legacy differently.

Legacy is not about what survives you; it is about what you leave in others while you are still here.

Legacy is the imprint of how you made people feel, the way your presence softened something hard, or helped someone see themselves more clearly.

If my life leaves behind anything, I hope that it is permission.

Permission for others to live honestly, to take up space, to rewrite the stories that no longer fit. I hope that it is a reminder that courage and kindness can coexist.

That strength can be soft.

That boundaries can be loving.

Quiet satisfaction has come for me from knowing that I have lived a life that truly feels mine.

Not perfect, nor easy, but deliberate.

Every choice, even the missteps, has taught me something vital.

I have learned to release the constant need for more, and instead ask:

Is this meaningful?

Does this align?

Does this add to my peace?

Because peace, I have found, is not passive.

Peace is the daily act of choosing what nourishes you and letting go of what does not.

Peace is the self-control of contentment.

Peace is not complacency.

Peace is clarity.

I no longer feel the need to rush toward the next thing. There is deep joy in stillness, in the slow unfolding of a normal day. I have grown comfortable with the in-between, the seasons of uncertainty, the pauses between achievements, the space where things are neither beginning nor ending, just becoming.

If I could tell my younger self anything, it would be this:

You were never behind.

Every detour, every heartbreak, every quiet act of courage was leading you here.

Trust the timing of your life. It unfolds exactly as it should.

I have spent years building a life that feels aligned with who I am, and now, I am learning to simply live it. To enjoy the fruit of all that striving. To laugh more, to rest more, to let joy be enough without the need to earn it.

Peace isn't found in doing everything right.

Peace is found in forgiving yourself when things go wrong.

Peace is knowing that growth doesn't always look like striving, pushing, forcing, hustling.

Sometimes, peace looks like softening. Sometimes, it looks like elegance.

As I look ahead, I no longer feel the need to prove, to perform, or to perfect. I just want to keep becoming, not someone new, but more deeply myself. To keep leading with truth, loving with intention, and living with gratitude.

This, to me, is the fairytale I never expected. It is not a story of rescue or arrival, but one of reclamation.

Learning that the real magic isn't found in the grand moments, but in the gentle, ordinary ones. The cup of coffee in the morning light. The laughter of people you love. The stillness that follows when you finally stop running from yourself.

The world told us to chase the fairytale, the castle, the crown, the promise of happily ever after.

But what I have learned is this: the magic isn't in the ending.

The magic is in the becoming.

And maybe that's sufficient.

A love letter to my younger self

Dear Kyles,

I know things might feel confusing or overwhelming right now, but I want you to know that you're going to be okay. You don't have to have it all figured out; nobody does.

Take your time to discover who you are and what truly matters to you.

You're going to face challenges, some that will shake your confidence and others that will teach you how strong you really are.

Don't be afraid to stand up for what's right, even if it feels lonely or scary.

Your values will be your compass.

Remember, it's okay to be imperfect.

You don't have to be anyone else but yourself, and that's enough.

Surround yourself with people who see and respect the real you; those relationships will be your greatest support.

Take moments to enjoy the little things, be kind to yourself, and don't rush the journey.

Life will bring you surprises, joy, heartbreak, and growth, but through it all, you'll become someone you're proud of.

Most importantly, trust yourself.

You are capable, worthy, and loved, exactly as you are.

With love.

Chapter 8:
Shrek…The Anti-Fairytale

Green Flags, Red Flags, and the Swamp in Between

If you are a single woman, by design, by choice, by fate, or by circumstance, I am damn sure you will have heard the term 'red flag', and I'm equally sure you will, 99% of the time, associate it with men.

These red flags are romanticised in fairytales: the swarthy villain, the cheeky trickster, or even the frog we are taught to kiss.

But in real life, red flags don't always wear a cape or carry a sword. Sometimes, they look like the people we love.

They can sound like your mother's guilt trips.

They can show up as a friend who only calls when they need rescuing.

They can look like a colleague who claims your work as their own, or a sibling who takes your kindness for granted.

They can even show up as your closest friends, subtly putting you in your place with their good intentions; tiny digs, manipulations, comparisons, or silences that leave you doubting yourself.

We are taught to recognise red flags as romantic danger signs: the emotionally unavailable guy, the ghoster, the love bomber.

But what if the real work is learning to spot them everywhere?

Because once you start seeing the pattern, you begin to understand it's not about them.

It's about what you have been taught to tolerate.

Most of us grew up believing that love, any love, is worth preserving. That 'family is everything.'

Good friends get infinite chances.

Being loyal means staying, putting up with bad behaviour, the moods, and the barbed comments.

Being the bigger person is important, and your feelings? Well, they don't matter at all.

But here's the thing: loyalty without boundaries is simply a recipe for losing yourself; it is a recipe for keeping you on a never-ending mousewheel of not feeling good enough, a recipe for walking on eggshells, doubting your choices, and spiralling into anxiety of your own making.

Why do I say 'your own making'?

Because my darling, when you accept these red flags as normal in your life, you are choosing to disrespect yourself.

Red flags are not just about men.

This chapter isn't about cynicism; it is about getting clear on what is right and good for you.

It is about learning that respect is the real fairytale, and that respect starts with how you treat yourself.

Because when you respect yourself deeply, when you honour yourself by treating yourself as you would others, something shifts.

Red flags don't always mean 'run', nor do they always mean 'put your walls up'.

Sometimes they mean 're-evaluate'.

This is a lesson I have learned the hard way: I was once upon a time the queen of walls, and it is something I work hard to dismantle.

I don't always succeed.

Should Shrek have put walls up around his swamp to keep people out?

Let's find out.

Mandy Merrifield

The Shrek Lens: The Anti-fairytale

Once upon a time, there was a green ogre who lived alone in a swamp. He didn't want company, he didn't want pity, and he definitely did not want to be saved.

He was doing just fine, thank you very much, until the world barged in with its expectations.

Sound familiar?

Maybe your swamp is your apartment, your career, your 'I'm fine' routine.

Maybe you, too, have spent years building walls around you. Maybe you built those walls to keep people out, and maybe you built them to protect your wellbeing and sanity. In my experience, people build walls to protect themselves.

I know I have.

When you have been judged, hurt, or exhausted enough times, aloneness can start to look like the only peace possible.

But then life throws you a Donkey.

Someone who won't leave you alone, no matter how many times you try to push them away.

Someone who challenges you.

Someone who forces you to look at how much of your independence is actually self-protection.

Shrek didn't go looking for adventure; it came barging through his door.

And that's often how growth happens: loud, annoying, inconvenient, and covered in mud.

What is the lesson here?

Aloneness can masquerade as peace, and it can work. There is a danger, though. Aloneness can very quickly lead to loneliness and disconnection, and it can make you think you're better off without people. This can slide into feeling unlovable and unwanted.

Often, this is far from the real truth.

But the walls you have created, brick by brick, hurt by hurt, fear by fear, the truth is that they don't protect you; they hide the love waiting on the other side.

The Princess Isn't What You Think

Let's talk about Fiona.

The girl in the tower.

The one cursed with imperfection.

By day, she is the fairytale version: pretty, polite, princess-perfect. By night, she turns into an ogre, the part of herself she hides from the world.

If that doesn't sum up the modern woman's double life, I don't know what does.

We've all been Fiona.

Performing 'fine' by day: capable, composed, competent; and all the while, our true, messy selves only come out in private. The part that is tired, angry, soft, hungry, vulnerable, frustrated, overworked, anxious, sad, lost, and all the other million adjectives that women use in secret, but struggle to say out loud, lest we be judged for not being enough, and not being able to handle it.

The fairytale told us love means being chosen for our best selves. The truth is, love begins when someone can handle your whole self.

When you stop hiding the ogre and start saying, "This is me, mud and all."

And when Shrek fell for Fiona, it wasn't because she fit a mould. It was because she didn't.

Because she was as weird, stubborn, and real as he was.

Mandy Merrifield

Beauty Was Never the Point

In Shrek, true love's kiss doesn't turn Fiona back into a human.

It reveals her real form. Her ogre form.

Let that sink in.

Her transformation isn't about becoming what the world expects. It is about becoming who she really is.

How many of us are still waiting for that moment? The one where we stop twisting ourselves into acceptable versions of what we think the world expects? The one where we realise maybe we were never meant to be the pretty princess in the story?

Maybe we were meant to build our own swamp. Not as a metaphorical exile, but a home. A space that fits us, not the other way around.

And maybe the people who truly love us will meet us there, not with a sword, a rescue plan, or a magic wand, but with the courage, honesty, and authenticity to sit in the mud beside us.

Shrek's swamp isn't glamorous.

It smells.

It's messy.

It's full of weird noises and questionable wildlife.

But it's also safe. Honest. Real.

And isn't that the truth?

That is what life is. Not a palace. Not perfection.

But a swamp. A beautiful, messy place you love, and have built on your terms.

Because that's where the magic actually happens.

Not in castles or crowns, but in the quiet space of knowing you're enough, even when you're muddy, grumpy, and unfiltered.

The Real 'Happily Ever After'

Did Shrek get his kingdom? No.

Did Fiona get a makeover? No.

There was no ball, no throne, no dramatic sunset ride (well, okay, maybe one).

Their 'ever after' was imperfect, loud, and completely theirs.

And maybe that's the point.

The fairytale says: You'll be happy when you're chosen.

The anti-fairytale says: You'll be happy when you choose yourself.

When you stop waiting for the rescue. When you stop pretending to be palatable. When you stop shrinking your ogre-sized truth to fit someone else's story.

Maybe you were never meant to be Cinderella.

Maybe you were always meant to be Fiona.

And maybe the swamp, the messy, glorious, unexpected life you have managed to build for yourself, maybe that was the fairytale all along.

The Fairytale Fix that Isn't

To make things even more complicated, Shrek has now entered our everyday world.

Somewhere between fairytales and dating apps, 'Shrekking' has become a thing, and no, it's not as cute as it sounds.

Shrekking describes a dating pattern where someone deliberately chooses a partner they perceive as beneath them, perhaps less attractive, less ambitious, or less socially desirable.

Let's say you see yourself as an 8/10 (and just for the record, what a terrible way to measure ourselves, girls), and you deliberately pick a 3, 4, or even a 5, because you believe it will be safer.

The thinking goes something like this:

'If I pick someone more available, they'll treat me better.'

'If I don't chase the handsome one, I won't get hurt.'

'If I choose someone who is not as in demand, they are less likely to dump me.'

Here's the ugly truth: lowering your standards doesn't guarantee emotional safety; it only guarantees self-betrayal.

The mindset behind 'Shrekking' isn't about genuine connection; it's about control.

It's trying to game the system of heartbreak.

But love doesn't work like that.

The real risk isn't dating someone out of your league.

The real risk is dating someone who doesn't meet you at your level: emotionally, energetically, or in how they value you.

Let's explore modern dating a little more for all the single girls out there.

Once upon a time, we were told to wait for the fairytale, to be patient, polite, and hopeful.

But what we got instead wasn't Prince Charming; it was breadcrumbing, gaslighting, life-boating, and the occasional Shrek pretending to be a saviour.

The modern dating world isn't a fairytale. It's a psychological obstacle course with emojis.

And yet, we still find ourselves playing the same old roles: the good girl, the fixer, the believer in potential.

But here's the truth: being the girl who believes in potential can be exhausting when your current Prince Charming has none.

Breadcrumbing: The Trail That Leads Nowhere

Once upon a time, Hansel and Gretel were lost in the woods.

To find their way home, they left a trail of breadcrumbs: small, comforting little promises that would lead them to safety, happiness, warmth, and cosiness.

But when they looked back, the trail was gone.

Eaten up.

And they realised they had been walking in circles all along.

Welcome to the modern dating world.

In dating, breadcrumbing is when someone gives you just enough attention to keep you interested, but never enough to build a real connection.

It's the 'Good morning' text that never becomes a plan.

It's the 'We should catch up sometime' message that never turns into an actual date.

It's the 'I miss you' that lands just when you've started to move on.

Breadcrumbers don't want to lose you, but they don't want to choose you either. They leave a trail, and you follow it, hoping it leads somewhere.

Hansel and Gretel weren't wrong to follow the breadcrumbs. They just didn't know the game was rigged.

Breadcrumbing preys on hope: that soft, human desire for connection, for things to mean something. It feeds on your patience, empathy, and belief that maybe this time it will be different.

The breadcrumber keeps you wandering in emotional limbo: not lost enough to walk away, but not fed enough to feel full.

And the truth is, sometimes we breadcrumb ourselves. We replay old messages, reread texts, interpret half-effort gestures as signs of fate.

A crumb feels better than nothing, right?

In the original fairytale, the trail of breadcrumbs leads to something that looks sweet: a house made of candy, shimmering with promise.

But inside waits a witch who feeds on lost souls.

That's breadcrumbing too: a sugar-coated illusion that drains your self-worth, one hit of attention at a time. You think you're in control, but the cycle feeds on your need to matter.

You wait for the next message, the next like, the next sliver of validation, the dopamine hit your mind, body, and nervous system crave. And the longer you stay in that forest, the harder it becomes to remember that you can walk out anytime.

The truth is, my darling girl, you don't need the crumbs.

You deserve the feast.

Gaslighting: The Mirror That Lies Back

Gaslighting is emotional manipulation disguised as reason.

Gaslighting is when someone twists the truth so subtly and so consistently that you begin to doubt your own memory, perception, and even sanity.

What does it sound like?

'I never said that.'

'You're overreacting.'

'You're remembering it wrong.'

'You're too sensitive.'

Slowly, you start to believe them.

You edit yourself down.

You second-guess your feelings.

You apologise for things that aren't yours to own.

Fuck the Fairytale: Find Your Own Magic

The term comes from a 1944 film, *Gaslight*.

The plot goes like this: a husband dims the lights and then denies it, repeatedly, until his wife questions her own mind.

But in real life, gaslighting doesn't need flickering lamps or dramatic scenes. It can come from a partner who calls you crazy when you catch them lying, a colleague who twists your words, or a family member who rewrites history to avoid accountability.

Gaslighting is quiet, persistent, and deeply corrosive.

Is there a fairytale that captures gaslighting perfectly?

Of course there is.

Fairytales often romanticise bad behaviour.

Take Snow White and the Evil Queen.

The Evil Queen is obsessed with being 'the fairest of them all.' She is the original manipulator wrapped in glamour. She stares into her mirror, demanding it affirm her version of reality.

And when it doesn't, she doesn't question herself; instead, she destroys the competition. She projects her own insecurities onto Snow White, reframing the young woman as a threat, a liar, an enemy.

That's the essence of gaslighting: it's not me, it's you.

The Queen can't face her fading power, so she builds an illusion of control, using deceit, disguise, and the mirror's reflection to protect her ego. Like so many gaslighters, she'd rather destroy the truth than face it.

Then comes the poisoned apple, the perfect metaphor for how gaslighting disguises harm as care.

The Queen doesn't force Snow White to take it; she offers it sweetly.

'I just want what's best for you.'

'You're misunderstanding me.'

'I didn't mean it like that.'

The poison is delivered through charm, apology, and false reassurance, and it is so convincing that you take a bite, hoping the sweetness means safety.

But the sweetness is the trap.

Gaslighting feeds on your hope, empathy, and belief in the good in people. By the time you realise it was never love, care, or truth, you've already swallowed it whole.

Life-Boating: The Little Mermaid Trap

Once upon a time, a mermaid fell in love with a man she'd barely spoken to.

She watched him from afar, imagined what it might feel like to be part of his world, then gave up her own, her home, her voice, her power, just to swim toward his.

And if that isn't the definition of life-boating, I don't know what is.

We romanticise her sacrifice, but really, it's a warning.

The Little Mermaid wasn't saving herself; she was surrendering.

Life-boating happens when you reach for a relationship, not because it's right, but because it feels like relief.

You're exhausted from keeping yourself afloat, from the loneliness, the uncertainty, the endless effort of being your own anchor.

Then someone drifts into your orbit, and suddenly they look like safety.

You call it love, but deep down, it's survival.

You're not stepping into a partnership; you're clinging to a raft.

It's the hope that someone else will carry the weight for a while, that being chosen will make the chaos feel calmer.

But all that does is put your peace in someone else's hands.

The Little Mermaid wasn't chasing connection; she was chasing escape.

From her own discomfort.

From feeling 'other.'

From the effort of standing alone in a world that didn't quite fit.

That's the hidden cost of life-boating: the quiet belief that someone else's ship will save you when your ocean feels too deep.

But lifeboats were never built for long voyages.

They are temporary by design: fragile, unstable, and dependent on calm seas.

The only way to survive is to stop looking for rescue and start learning how to swim in your own tide.

The Ultimate Rewrite

Every time you walk away from a red flag, you rewrite your story.

You stop being the girl waiting in the tower, and start being the woman who built her own home.

You don't have to burn the fairytale, just stop starring in someone else's.

Find Your Own Magic: A Guided Reflection

You're Not the Damsel. You're the Damn Storyline

Build From Worth, Not Wounds

When you look at your relationships, past or present, be honest: were you loving from strength or survival?

Were you hoping to be chosen, or already standing in your own choice?

The energy you bring is the energy that sets the tone.

If it's coming from fear, it'll always feel like chasing.

If it's coming from worth, it'll feel like peace, even when you're alone.

Reflection:

- What does it feel like in your body when you act from self-worth versus self-doubt?

- Where have you mistaken attention for affection, or stability for safety?

- What would choosing yourself look like today, in action, not just in theory?

Boundaries Are the New Fairytale Ending

You don't need to scream your worth to be seen; you just need to stop handing it away.

Boundaries aren't walls; they're filters. They keep the noise out so you can hear your own truth again.

If someone gets upset by your boundaries, that's proof they were benefiting from your lack of them.

Reflection:

- Where are you over-explaining, over-apologising, or over-functioning?

- What line could you draw right now that would make life feel lighter?

- What would it mean to say simply, "that doesn't work for me", and leave it at that?

Walking Away Is Self-Respect in Motion

When someone's words and actions don't match, that's not confusion; it's information.

You don't need closure, a grand goodbye, or an apology that may never come.

You just need the courage to stop trying to prove your value to someone who's already shown they can't see it.

Reflection:

- What story do you tell yourself about why you can't leave, whether that be a friendship or a relationship?

- How many times have you mistaken potential for partnership?

- What would change if you decided that self-respect was more important than being chosen?

Stop Accepting 'Almosts'

Almost loved. Almost respected. Almost seen.

Half-effort is still half-empty, no matter how you dress it up.

The bare minimum is not romance; it's emotional rationing.

You deserve someone who meets you in the middle, not someone who keeps you on the edge.

Reflection:

- Where are you settling for scraps and calling it connection?

- What's the real cost of staying small so someone else can stay comfortable?

- What would it look like to only match energy, never chase it again?

Rewrite the Story: You're the Author Now

You don't need a rescuer. You need a pen.

Saying 'Fuck the fairytale' doesn't mean love isn't real; it means you're done mistaking rescue for romance.

You're writing a better story now: one where the heroine saves herself, builds her peace, and loves from overflow, not emptiness.

Reflection:

- If you stopped waiting for someone to save you, what would you finally do for yourself?

- What's your version of 'happily ever after', and how does it feel when you picture it?

- What chapter are you ready to start writing next?

Chapter 9:
Mandy, This Is Me

I live on my own.

With my dog, Ivy.

She is a small, spoilt little thing with a heart bigger than she knows, and in every way, she is my anchor. She keeps me grounded, forces me out of the house when I would rather stay curled up, and has an uncanny ability to sense when my heart feels a little too heavy.

Ivy doesn't care whether I've achieved enough that day, whether my apartment is neat, or whether my life looks the way it is supposed to. She simply wants to be with me, and to be loved, and that quiet companionship is often enough.

I have two daughters, one who lives a long way away, and the other who hasn't spoken to me in over five years. That last sentence still catches in my throat every time I write it. It is not something I say for sympathy; it is simply a fact of my life, one that has shaped me more deeply than I could ever explain.

I love them both fiercely.

Even in the silence, the love doesn't disappear. It just shifts shape.

I work hard. I study a lot. I try new things, and I do my best to live my life with purpose and meaning. Some days, that drive feels clear; other days, it feels like I'm fumbling my way through the dark, trying to find the light switch. But I keep going. I keep learning. I keep trying to be a little better, a little braver, a little more myself.

So, am I living my fairytale?

No. Definitely not.

Interesting, isn't it?

If that's the case, then why on earth am I qualified to write this book? And how on earth do I have the gall to tell you to design the life of your dreams?

Well, that's the thing about qualifications, they're not always about credentials or perfect stories.

Is anyone really qualified to write a book?

At the end of the day, a book is imagination, opinion, experience, interpretation, wrapped up in a bit of craft, some good editing, a few punchy one-liners, maybe a laugh or two, a touch of heartache, and a title that makes you stop long enough to read the back cover.

So let me tell you a little of my story.

My dad died last year. We always had a pretty complicated relationship, never outright cruel, but distant, tangled, and often misunderstood. And this is going to sound awful, but when I was younger, back in those teenage years when I thought I knew everything, I thought I was better than him.

I was wrong.

In his final years, and particularly in his final week, we became closer. There was a softness that came in when the fight went out of both of us. We started to understand each other, maybe for the first time.

"I fucked up a bit, Dad," I said to him, as we were saying our goodbyes on his final day, both of us fighting, and failing to keep the tears at bay.

"You did alright mate," he replied. It might not sound like much, but that was high praise, respect and love from my dad, in the only way he knew how.

With those words, he summed up my story in a nutshell.

For all the mistakes I've made, and there have been plenty, I would like to think that I have learned from them.

There isn't a one-size-fits-all solution for life.

Fuck the Fairytale: Find Your Own Magic

There is no manual, no universal script that applies to every human being on the planet.

When we think about fairytales and girls, and the lives we were taught to build, maybe that's what this book is really about: working out which parts of the script fit, and which parts are up to you to rewrite.

For me, the role of wife didn't work.

Nor did I want to remain in my hometown.

And the idea of spending decades in the same job, clocking in and clocking out while life slowly ticked away, that wasn't for me either.

That doesn't make those things wrong. It just means they weren't my version of right.

And what I've learned, through years of trial and error, of building and breaking and rebuilding again, is that it's okay for that to be the case.

Mum is a role I work on every day. Some days I feel like I'm halfway to nailing it. Other days, not so much. Have you heard the saying 'children don't come with an instruction manual'?

Never a truer statement has been made.

But what no one tells you is that you don't come with one either.

Maternal instinct isn't something that comes naturally to every woman. I am one of those women.

I love my girls. They are the loves of my life. But I have never been the kind of woman who coos over babies or goes weak at the sight of a newborn. The children in my orbit, my nephews, for example, get big, warm Aunty love when I have access to give it to them, but no one would ever describe me as clucky.

I never have been.

And for a long time, I thought that made me defective, or cold, or somehow less of a woman.

Do I sound like a monster?

Maybe to some.

I beg to differ.

And this, this right here, is precisely what I'm talking about in this book.

You can stand tall and be you in whatever way that presents itself.

You do not have to apologise for the things you don't want, the instincts you don't have, or the paths that do not fit you. You do not have to perform womanhood according to the script you were handed at birth.

You are allowed to define your own version of enough. Your own version of happy.

Your own fairytale, one that doesn't require a castle, a prince, or a perfectly curated life.

Because maybe, just maybe, the most beautiful thing we can do as women is to stop pretending we have to want what everyone else does, and start living the story that feels true to us.

Find Your Own Magic: A Guided Reflection

What Does Freedom Look Like for You?

Name your version of freedom.

Close your eyes and imagine a life where you feel completely free.

Here are some thought starters:

- What does a day in your life look like if you don't have to please anyone?

- Who do you spend time with, and who do you limit or let go?

- What work, habits, or routines feel liberating instead of draining?

- How does your body feel, your mind feel, your heart feel in this version of freedom?

- Now, translate that vision into real steps.

Use this scaffolding if you like:

- What is one boundary you can set this week to protect your time, energy, or emotional space?

- What is one thing you can stop doing that doesn't serve your freedom (habit, social obligation, relationship dynamic)?

- What's one small act of courage you can take this week that aligns with your freedom vision, for example, saying no, investing in yourself, or leaving a toxic situation?

- How can you celebrate even small wins towards living your freedom fully?

Chapter 10:
The Black Dog

On my darkest days, she helps me out of bed.

When I am sad, she makes me smile.

When I feel like the world is against me, and I will never be able to outrun the past, she offers herself up for a cuddle.

She is my little black dog.

And she is not the fucker that runs around in my head.

That black dog doesn't take up as much space as it used to, but it still appears from time to time.

What is 'the black dog', you ask?

My darling, it is depression.

Crippling, can't-move, concrete bands strangling your body, your mind, your heart.

Nothingness.

Desolation.

Black.

And it is something I have battled on and off for most of my life.

It wasn't spoken about much when I was growing up. While mental health wasn't a taboo topic, it was simply one that rarely came up. It certainly wasn't as visible as it is today.

Thank the universe it is no longer this way.

Because it kills.

I am not an expert in mental health, even though I have been in therapy for years. And while I speak about it openly, I am not a practitioner.

So please, read this chapter as a personal account only, and if you resonate, nod, or identify with what I am about to share, please seek professional help. At the back of this book is a list of resources available in Australia. Please use them.

Ivy.

My little black dog. I love her so.

She is a schnauzer cross poodle, and she is the lady of the house in our relationship.

Every morning I wake to her on the satin pillow next to me, and every day I say: "How lucky are we to have each other?"

And we are.

There is no dog I know who is more pampered and more loved, but in the same sentence, I know that is not entirely true. My many pooch-parent friends love their angels just as much as I love mine.

Ivy came into my life in October 2017, at just eight weeks old. She was so tiny, she fitted into the palm of my hand.

Choosing her was purposeful.

I, absolutely, deliberately, chose to purchase a black dog.

In October 2017, just a year sober, I still had days when I couldn't get out of bed. Mostly weekends, as I had returned to the workforce and some semblance of routine had re-entered my life.

That did not mean that the minute I got home from work in the evening, I didn't climb under the doona and try to wish the world away.

I did.

I was sober, sure.

But I was still broke as hell, trying to get back on my feet, working odd jobs to pay for my groceries, and catching a bus to work because I couldn't afford the $10-a-day parking fees in the city.

I was a long way from the nice, once supposedly happy wife and mother who lived in the beautifully renovated home in the nice part of town.

No matter what I seemed to do, I couldn't get my relationships back on track with my daughters, and I realise now that I was expecting too much, too soon. I couldn't recognise that at the time, and I felt sorry for myself.

Miserable, in fact.

And so I hid.

Putting myself to bed has always been my crutch. The narrative in my head went something like this:

'If I go to sleep, maybe when I wake in a few hours, I will feel better.'

'If I go to sleep, maybe when I wake, there will be a message waiting for me on my phone from one of the girls.'

'If I go to sleep, at least a couple of hours will have passed where I haven't had to think about the shit-show my life has become.'

And… 'maybe when I wake up, everything will be okay.'

Ha.

You cannot move forward without action, and I was actively staying still.

I needed a reset. Something to break the cycle.

A puppy.

Ha.

What a reset she was.

From the minute I collected her from the breeder and held her close to my heart, she has done exactly what I needed her to do.

Love me unconditionally. Get me out of bed.

Vertical is her preferred status of Mandy.

Take her for a walk. Admit to her that she has won when she pulls out yet another plant I have potted.

Fuck the Fairytale: Find Your Own Magic

Feed her. Run around after her and retrieve my favourite shoe from her mouth.

Rub her belly. Admonish her with a laugh when she chews the arms and back of my sofa.

Give her the toilet roll when it is empty; yes, she has to come with me when I use the bathroom. She has an uncanny knack for knowing when the last sheet of tissue comes off the cardboard… she races in, grabs it, and spends ten minutes nugging on it before losing interest and moving on.

Immediately upon waking, give her treats from her 'lolly cupboard'. Not her breakfast… no, no. Treats first, breakfast second. If I dare do it in any other order, she looks at me like I'm on crack.

When finishing a meal, no matter if it is my yoghurt and fruit breakfast, or my microwave dinner, she knows when the fork or spoon is scraping the last morsels from the plate, and she is waiting. And for those of you grossed out by me letting my pooch lick my plate, that's fine. You don't need to eat at my home, and I'm okay with that.

When my girls were little, I used to put their bottles in the dishwasher to sterilise them. I was told by the recognised authority at the time that dishwasher sterilisation was perfectly fine, and that we didn't need all the expensive accessories and machines from the big baby warehouse megastores marketed as essential. Young mums are so incredibly vulnerable, wanting to do the right thing and afraid of not having what Instagram and Pinterest tell them they should have, that babies become a multi-million-dollar industry.

I digress.

Ivy licks my plate, and then it goes in the dishwasher. Sterilised. Done.

Where did her name come from?

I wanted to call her Olive. I heard a line in a movie once: *Easy A* with Emma Stone, when she introduces herself, she says, "Olive, it is an anagram of 'I love'".

So that was who my little black dog would be.

My youngest daughter had a different idea. For some unknown reason, she was obsessed with Beyoncé at the time. "We are calling her Beyoncé mum," she announced to me on one of the rare occasions we spoke back in 2017.

An emphatic "no way" was my immediate response.

"Blue Ivy then," she countered. For those of you uneducated Queen B non-fan-girls out there, Blue Ivy is Bey's daughter.

The compromise was Ivy. I was able to get Olive in as her middle name.

And because I would have literally walked on hot coals to try and assuage my guilt at being an alcoholic, for ruining my daughters' lives, for destroying their childhood, and for disappointing them… even though I was lucky to see or speak to my youngest daughter once every second month, I allowed her to name my puppy.

Whoa.

Mandy.

Listen to yourself.

I know you can see it, so let's call it out.

I am hard on myself. Exceptionally so.

My rational, logical brain now knows I wasn't the only one at fault in the breakdown of my marriage. I also know that alcoholism is a disease. My ex-husband made choices too; they are not my story to tell.

I do own my part, though, and it is a big one. In the same breath, I acknowledge that it is not all my fault. There are still plenty of people who can't or don't want to see that.

Ce la vie.

You see, when you are an alcoholic, it is big, it is a glaringly obvious target to point at, and it is something that, even when you are knocking on the door of a decade sober, people will still use against you.

And they do.

And I have learned to roll with it.

Some days, I wonder whether people will ever see the person I am today, and sadly, I know that for some people, they never will.

I have had to accept that. It hurts.

There is no time machine. I wish I could change it.

I can't.

All I can do is try to be the best version of myself every day. Some days I succeed, and some days I do not.

Depression.

I think it will always be there to some extent. I have learnt to manage it.

Ivy has an enormous amount to do with that.

I remember a couple of months before I got sober; I lay on the floor for at least three days, immobile, unable to function. The floor was cold, I couldn't remember the last time I had a shower, and I remember that I faintly smelt. My hair was falling out, and my skin was peeling off.

That was the worst of it. Looking back at all the bouts of depression I have had in my life, I cannot recall an episode worse than that one.

I cannot imagine the worry I put my parents through.

Like most people with an alcohol problem, or any other addiction for that matter, I was very good at hiding it. Although at this point, I think my mum, in particular, was realising something was very wrong.

She had no idea of the enormity of it. No one did.

I excel at most things I do, and being an alcoholic was one of them. Hiding it was another.

So for three days, when I didn't answer the phone to tens of calls, I can't imagine what I put my mum through. I'm sure she didn't know whether I was alive or dead, but I am also very good at putting walls up. And so, because of previous tensions in our relationship, she knew well enough not to turn up at my door.

It must have been hell.

Another thing I will never forgive myself for. As a mum myself, I now understand what that must have felt like.

Those three days.

Desolation.

Except for the thought that the world and all the people in it would be better off without me.

I didn't do it.

Do you want to know why?

Because my daughters were the only ones who had keys to my house. And I didn't want to ruin their lives even more by having them find me.

Pretty tough stuff to hear, huh?

This book is about real life, warts and all, and for so many people out there, this is a part of their real lives too.

And so, I share. Not for you to feel sorry for me, certainly not for accolades, and most importantly, not to excuse what happened.

I do not share to be performative. I share to bring awareness. That the sun does come up, and life does go on.

You can make life as fabulous as you want it to be. And the world would definitely not be better without you.

My angel, my little black dog, my Ivy Olive, she saved my life. She brings joy to my days and love to my heart. And most importantly, she keeps that other black dog at bay.

Most of us have been told angels have wings; some of us have learned they have paws.

Chapter 11:
Truth is a Perspective

The words that follow are from the perspective of your author.

I urge you, my darling girl, please, go ahead and choose your own perspective, the one that feels true to you, that sits comfortably in your centre, and that aligns with the woman you know deep down you truly are.

Truth isn't universal.

Truth is perspective.

It is a lens that reveals reality from the point in time you are in, from the direction you are looking, and from the mindset you are carrying in that moment.

If you grew up fed on fairytales, rom-coms, glossy magazines, or, more recently, social media, you have very likely inherited a lens that wasn't designed to help you live a life that perfectly suits you.

This chapter isn't here to criticise those stories. It's here to examine the lens they gave you and to offer something far more honest and liberating.

It starts with one question:

What lens are you looking through?

Fairytales Aren't Dangerous. The Lenses They Create Are

Every fairytale delivers a worldview before it delivers a plot.

Snow White teaches softness.

Cinderella teaches endurance.

Ariel teaches self-sacrifice.

And those worldviews stick. They become the lens women look through long into adulthood.

A few examples you'll recognise:

- You stay in a draining job because you should be grateful.

- You explain your feelings softly, carefully, so you won't don't upset someone.

- You apologise before expressing a need.

- You cling to potential instead of proof of behaviour.

- You settle for crumbs, and you call it connection.

Not because you're weak, unwise, or unaware, but because the lenses you inherited rewarded those behaviours.

But imagine if our heroines had lived their own truth, not the one written for them.

Snow White: The Truth of the Poisoned Apple

Snow White saw the best in everyone, even the woman who wanted her dead.

She shrank herself for safety. She cleaned, nurtured, and softened every edge she had.

This is the same lens modern women use when they:

- Ignore red flags because 'he means well.'

- Stay connected to toxic family members out of obligation.

- Downplay their discomfort to avoid appearing dramatic or needy.

- Rationalise someone's hurtful behaviour because 'they've had a hard life.'

But imagine Snow White living her truth instead.

She would have recognised danger without sugarcoating it.

She would have walked away from the dwarves' emotional reliance instead of becoming their unpaid therapist.

She would have trusted her intuition over politeness.

She wouldn't have stayed in the forest waiting for rescue; she would have found her own path out.

Snow White, living her truth, is the woman who stops making excuses for others and starts protecting her peace. She calls out red flags, trusts her intuition, and puts herself in charge of her wellbeing and her future.

Cinderella: The Truth of the Glass Slipper

Cinderella endured mistreatment because she was told that patience equals virtue, and virtue equals reward.

This lens is still alive today.

Modern women channel Cinderella when they:

- Stay at jobs where they are overlooked because 'loyalty matters.'

- Remain in relationships long past the point of respect.

- Carry the emotional labour at home without question.

- Tell themselves it will get better 'after the next milestone.'

- Wait for someone else to change so they can finally be happy themselves.

But imagine Cinderella living her truth.

Would she have waited for the fairy godmother? No.

Would she have stayed out of loyalty to those who delighted in treating her like a piece of crap? Uh…. I don't think so.

She would have left that cluster-fuck of a situation with her skills, wit, and courage and rebuilt a life on her own terms.

She would have seen that leaving is not failure.

It is self-respect.

Cinderella, living her truth, is the woman who stops mistaking endurance for strength. She puts boundaries in place and respects the hell out of herself.

Ariel: The Truth of the Seashell

Ariel's story is the most modern of all: the woman with passions, curiosity, ambition, and a belief that she must change entirely to be loved.

Women still hand over their voice in subtle everyday ways:

- Silencing opinions to keep the peace in a relationship.

- Minimising their accomplishments so a partner, friend or colleague won't feel intimidated.

- Morphing into the version of themselves they think others want.

- Abandoning interests, goals, or friendships to fit into someone else's world.

- Shrinking desires to seem 'easy going.'

If Ariel lived her truth?

She would've explored both worlds without giving up her identity.

She would've kept her voice, literally and metaphorically.

She would've chosen a partner who valued her curiosity, not one attracted to her silence.

She would've realised that real love expands you; it does not compress you.

Ariel, living her truth, is the woman who refuses to become smaller for connection.

How Lenses Shape Your Everyday Reality

To bring this closer to home, here's how the wrong lens can distort truths today:

Scenario 1: He Pulls Away

Fairytale lens: I must have done something wrong.

Truth lens: His behaviour is information, not a commentary on my worth.

Scenario 2: You Want a Raise

Fairytale lens: I should wait until they notice my hard work.

Truth lens: Advocating for myself is necessary, not needy.

Scenario 3: A Friendship Drifts

Fairytale lens: What can I fix?

Truth lens: Not every connection is meant to last forever.

Scenario 4: You're Tired of Being the Strong One

Fairytale lens: I should carry it alone.

Truth lens: Strength is asking for support.

Scenario 5: You Outgrow a Relationship

Fairytale lens: But we've invested so much time.

Truth lens: Long-term attachment is not a reason to stay small.

Scenario 6: Someone Treats You Poorly

Fairytale lens: Maybe they're just struggling.

Truth lens: Their struggle does not excuse mistreatment.

These moments aren't about what happens; they're about how you interpret what happens.

And your interpretation is your lens. That means it's yours to change.

You Didn't Choose Your First Lens, But You Can Choose the Next One

Your first lens was built from:

- Childhood roles

- Cultural expectations

- Early heartbreaks

- Unspoken rules around being a 'good girl'

- Fear of disappointing others

- Survival strategies

- Generational patterns

- The quiet pressure to remain agreeable

The problem isn't that you had these lenses. It's that no one told you you're allowed to update them.

A cracked lens doesn't mean your life is falling apart. It means your life is trying to expand.

The Lenses You Grow Into

When a woman chooses a new lens, she becomes impossible to manipulate, by others or by her old patterns.

These are the lenses women often grow into:

- **The Reality Lens:** You see behaviour for what it is, not what it could be.

- **The Boundaries Lens:** You stop explaining limits and start enforcing them.

- **The Desire Lens:** You want things openly, without apology.

- **The Self-Respect Lens:** Bare minimums no longer impress you.

- **The Expansion Lens:** You choose the life that stretches you, not the one that shrinks you.

This is where truth becomes empowerment.

Find Your Own Magic: A Guided Reflection

The Final Question That Changes Everything

Truth is a perspective. It is the lens you choose to look through.

Not the one handed to you by childhood. Not the one carved by fairytales. The one you choose now.

So ask yourself: "What lens am I looking through today?"

And even more importantly: "What lens would I choose if I lived the truth for me, not what conditioning has taught me to see as reality?"

Once you answer that, the rest of your life rearranges itself around the woman you were always meant to be.

It is here, in this space, that you get to design your own life and find your own magic.

A letter to my younger self

Dear Mandy

I know it's hard right now, honey.

I know you don't feel like you fit in.

It's not fair.

And it's shit.

I get it.

But it won't always be this way, I promise you.

You've still got a long road ahead, and that road is going to test you more than you can ever imagine.

But you know what?

You are fucking strong.

You are a fighter, and you will never give up.

You have two beautiful girls who will come into your life, and even though you probably won't fully appreciate what that means at the time, as you get older and wiser, you will understand they are your greatest achievement.

Will those girls test you?

Yes.

Will you disappoint them and make mistakes along the way?

Yes.

Do you regret motherhood?

Not for one single second. You will hear yourself say, often:

"I love every single hair on their head."

And no matter what happens, you will be so thankful that you get to be their mum, even if at times they don't want you.

Will you make other mistakes?

Yes.

Will you chase the wrong men?

Yes.

Will you hurt people?

Yes.

Will you lose people along the way?

Yes.

But you will learn.

You will learn to love yourself, for all your flaws, and more importantly, for all your fabulousness.

You will learn that walls are not the answer, and that the word 'fine' is one of the most dangerous in the English-speaking language.

You will learn that sometimes the expectations you thought were placed on your shoulders by others were actually expectations you put there yourself. And you are allowed to just be you.

You will find the family that matters, that loves you no matter what.

You will come out the other side.

Bruised, and in some ways, a bit emotionally worse for wear.

There is a reason you are here. Remember that.

You will write a book that will inspire countless women to design their own lives, and to learn to love themselves, just as you have learned to love yourself.

That book will change lives.

As your dad will say to you when he leaves this world, 'You did alright, mate.'

And you do.

Love, an older and wiser Mandy x

...and on her own fucking terms,

she lived

Happily Ever After

The Women Behind The Words

To the incredible women who shared their stories in *F*ck the Fairytale: Find Your Own Magic*

You are ordinary, everyday women, and that's exactly what makes what you've done extraordinary. You showed up with honesty and vulnerability at a depth most people never share, especially in a world obsessed with curated boxes and filtered perfection. The world needs more of this, more truth, more realness, more women willing to speak openly about the parts of life that actually shape us.

Your generosity in sharing the unpolished, honest parts of your story, your willingness to open the door on moments most people keep hidden behind the highlight reel, has created something far bigger than any of us could have built alone. This book exists because you trusted yourself, trusted your voice, and trusted me enough to let your truth be seen.

I am deeply grateful for your courage, your openness, and the impact your stories will have on women who are tired of pretending and ready for something real.

Thank you.

All of my love,

Mandy

The Women Behind The Words

Guin

Guinevere (Guin) Dickie, 41, lives in the tight-knit town of Manildra, NSW, a community of just 500 people, with her husband and their three children: a 12-year-old daughter from her first marriage, and a 7-year-old daughter and 3-year-old son from her second. Navigating the unique challenge of raising children at three very different life stages, preschool, primary school and high school, Guin balances her family life with a career that moves between maternity and other short-term contracts, embracing the flexibility and variety her work brings.

A former roller derby player, Guin has traded the skates for a life of walking, cooking and volunteering, finding joy in the simple pleasures and meaningful contributions to her community. She describes herself as settled, calm and satisfied, appreciating the balance she has built in her life and the warmth of close connections with family, friends and her small-town surroundings.

You can find Guin here:

https://www.linkedin.com/in/guin-dickie

Sahar

Sahar is a Canberra-based public sector leader and creative storyteller whose work bridges governance, global experience and personal expression. With a career spanning policy, project management and governance, she brings clarity, compassion and strategic depth to every role she takes on.

Beyond public service, Sahar shares her voice through her radio show, preserving the language by connecting the community through authentic conversations. Her food blog celebrates culture and connection through vibrant, memory-rich meals, while her fashion page empowers women to embrace style as a form of self-expression.

Whether she's shaping systems or styling stories, Sahar leads with mindfulness, creativity and a belief that real impact begins with living in alignment. Sahar lives in Canberra with her husband and two children.

You can find Sahar here:

Radio: https://www.cmsradio.org.au/shows/urdu-program/

Blog: https://www.instagram.com/whatscookingsahar/

Fashion: https://www.instagram.com/whatstrendingsahar/

Angela

*Angela, 62, lives in Sydney and is happily retired. She is married for the second time and the proud mother of three adult children, aged 37, 35 and 30. Passionate about family, Angela loves spending time with her grandchildren, travelling and singing.

A lifelong learner, she didn't attend university until she was 36, proving it's never too late to follow your dreams and expand your horizons. Angela describes herself as curious, warm and full of life, embracing new experiences while cherishing the joys of family and personal growth.

Angela has generously shared her experience, choosing to stay anonymous

Cleo

*Cleo, 28, is a Sydney-based outdoors enthusiast with a love for fly fishing, shooting and CrossFit. Currently between jobs and exploring new opportunities, she brings a grounded resilience and curiosity to whatever comes next. Single and without children, she fills her days with adventure, movement and time spent outdoors, especially on the water.

A memorable recent highlight in Cleo's life was being featured alongside her mother in a Japanese fly-fishing magazine. Together, they advocated for greater visibility and inclusion of women in the sport, a cause Cleo is passionate about. Their story not only showcased their shared bond but also encouraged more women to discover the joy and empowerment that come from casting a line.

Cleo has generously shared her experience, choosing to stay anonymous

Rachel

Rachel Brown, 56, is a full-time entrepreneur who recently traded city life for the sunny shores of Paradise Point on the Gold Coast – yippee!

Living with her partner and the proud mother of four grown sons ranging from 28 to 21, Rachel balances family, work and play with energy and joy. Twice divorced, she approaches life with resilience, humour and a readiness to embrace every new adventure.

A former principal dancer with the Alice Springs Ballet Company, Rachel has always lived with passion and discipline, whether on stage or in her entrepreneurial ventures. She keeps her body moving through the gym and her mind inspired by stories, currently lost in Karin Slaughter's gripping *Will Trent* series on Audible.

Rachel's life is a vibrant mix of creativity, curiosity and connection. She celebrates each day with gratitude, laughter and a zest for discovering all that life has to offer.

You can find Rachel here:

Facebook: https://www.facebook.com/share/1C95Ex1xpQ/

Instagram:
https://www.instagram.com/rachel.brown1010?igsh=MTVheWRxcGw1eWpoZg==

Eira

*Eira is a 32-year-old Senior Development Planner living in Canberra. She is partnered, previously divorced, and enjoys an active, health-focused lifestyle that includes running, walking, gym sessions and travelling whenever she can. Diagnosed with type 1 diabetes at the age of seven, Eira has grown up with resilience, determination and a strong sense of self-discipline.

Known for her passion and drive, Eira strives to be a loyal and caring friend and partner. She has a thoughtful approach to life, always looking for something to be grateful for each day. Whether tackling her professional goals, exploring new places or challenging herself physically, she approaches life with energy, curiosity and a commitment to living intentionally.

Eira has generously shared her experience, choosing to stay anonymous

Sophia

*Sophia lives on the outskirts of Sydney with her husband and their two children, a 15-year-old daughter and a 7-year-old son. She is an NLP-certified life coach and a filmmaker, blending her professional creativity with her dedication to family life. Sophia's work focuses on empowering women, helping them to navigate the challenges of life with confidence, clarity and self-compassion.

Outside of work, Sophia enjoys dancing, gym sessions, long scenic drives, spa days, listening to music and sipping coffee in cafés surrounded by nature. She grew up multilingual, often mixing three languages in one conversation, a skill she took for granted until meeting others, and it has shaped her adaptable, curious and open-minded approach to life.

Fun fact: she could happily live on honey alone!

Sophia brings energy, warmth and creativity to everything she does, balancing her professional pursuits with a rich and joyful family life.

Sophia has generously shared her experience, choosing to stay anonymous

Kyles

*Kyles, in her mid-40s, is an HR Generalist. Married and without children, she embraces an active lifestyle, enjoying mountain biking, hiking, snow skiing, listening to music and travelling. Always planning her next adventure, Kyles balances her professional life with a love of exploration and new experiences.

Known for her happy and bubbly nature, Kyles is grounded in her values and guided by a strong moral compass. Loyal, kind and honest, she cares deeply for family and friends, yet is unafraid to challenge the status quo or speak bluntly when needed. With a clear sense of self and her place in the world, Kyles lives by the principle of working to live, not living to work, embracing life with curiosity, courage and joy.

Kyles has generously shared her experience, choosing to stay anonymous

Meet The Author:
Mandy

Mandy grew up in a small town as the eldest of three children. Born with complex health challenges and facing difficult physical issues during her teenage years, she often struggled with feelings of inadequacy.

In a nutshell, she never felt 'good enough.'

Today, she embraces her body as fabulously unique, having only one working lung and having worn a back brace for scoliosis, which made her childhood both restrictive and emotionally taxing. These experiences stayed with her into adulthood.

By 2016, Mandy hit rock bottom, battling alcoholism and losing almost everything. The day she got sober, she had $1.17 to her name. Through that dark period, she found the resilience to rebuild her life and now channels her experiences into helping others design their own lives, build confidence and cultivate balance and a grounded sense of self.

Having faced years of deep depression while navigating challenging family dynamics, Mandy understands the strength it takes to live openly and authentically. By sharing her journey, she hopes to offer a story that might inspire, comfort or simply remind someone they're not alone.

Mandy Merrifield

With over 20 years of corporate leadership experience in emotional intelligence, organisational culture and learning and development, Mandy brings both professional expertise and deep personal insight to her coaching. Divorced and a mother of two adult daughters, she lives in Brisbane with her beloved pooch.

Mandy is an Executive Coach with postgraduate qualifications in organisational development and leadership, a qualified hypnotherapist, Master Neuro-Linguistic Practitioner and TimeLine Therapist. She has also studied positive psychology and Acceptance and Commitment Therapy.

When she isn't writing or coaching, you will find her walking with her little black dog Ivy, along the Brisbane River, heading to the gym or hanging out with a friend for morning coffee. She will probably be dreaming up her next adventure, which in 2026 is to hike the Camino de Santiago from Portugal to Spain.

Today, Mandy works one-on-one with women to navigate societal pressures and expectations with compassion and clarity, empowering them to live lives aligned with their own values and desires rather than what anyone else says they 'should' do.

www.mandymerrifield.org

Black Dog Institute

I've chosen to donate 10% of all profits from this book to the Black Dog Institute, a cause close to my heart because of my own experiences with mental health, and because of the compassion and support their work brings to so many. Contributing in this way is a small gesture of gratitude and hope, a way of giving back to a community that quietly holds so many of us through the times when life feels overwhelming.

Their research, education and support make a real difference in people's lives, and I'm humbled to be able to contribute, even in a small way.

Please note that while a portion of the proceeds will support the Black Dog Institute, they do not endorse this book, nor should it be considered a mental health resource.

www.blackdoginstitute.org.au

Emergency Numbers

Emergency services | 000

Lifeline | 13 11 14

Kids Helpline | 1800 55 1800

Suicide Callback Service | 1300 659 467

www.ingramcontent.com/pod-product-compliance
Lightning Source LLC
Chambersburg PA
CBHW040524170726
48295CB00012B/333